DIRTY FEET

EDEM AWUMEY

DIRTY FEET

TRANSLATED FROM THE FRENCH BY LAZER LEDERHENDLER

ANANSI

First published as *Les pieds sales* in 2009 by Les Éditions du Boréal.
First published in English in 2011 by House of Anansi Press Inc.

This edition published in 2011 by
House of Anansi Press Inc.
110 Spadina Avenue, Suite 801
Toronto, ON, M5V 2K4
Tel. 416-363-4343 Fax 416-363-1017
www.anansi.ca

Distributed in Canada by
HarperCollins Canada Ltd.
1995 Markham Road
Scarborough, ON, M1B 5M8
Toll free tel. 1-800-387-0117

Distributed in the United States by
Publishers Group West
1700 Fourth Street
Berkeley, CA 94710
Toll free tel. 1-800-788-3123

House of Anansi Press is committed to protecting our natural environment.
As part of our efforts, this book is printed on paper that contains 100%
post-consumer recycled fibres, is acid-free, and is processed chlorine-free.

An excerpt from the draft of this translation was previously published
in the online journal *Carte Blanche*.

The epigraph is from a poem by Mahmoud Darwish titled in English "My father." The
translation is by A. M. Elmessiri and can be found in *The Palestinian Wedding: A Bilingual
Anthology of Contemporary Palestinian Resistance Poetry*, collected and translated by A. M.
Elmessiri (Washington, D.C.: Three Continents Press, 1982).

The excerpt on page 156 is from the poem "Birds Die in Galilee" by
Mahmoud Darwish, translated by Denys Johnson-Davies, and can be found in
The Music of Human Flesh, a collection of poems by Darwish selected and translated by
Denys Johnson-Davies (Washington, D.C.: Three Continents Press, 1980).

15 14 13 12 11 1 2 3 4 5

Library and Archives Canada Cataloguing in Publication

Awumey, Edem,
[Pieds sales. English]
Dirty feet / Edem Awumey ; translated by Lazer Lederhendler.

Translation of: Les pieds sales.
ISBN 978-0-88784-244-3

I. Lederhendler, Lazer. II. Titre. III. Titre: Pieds sales. English.

PS8609.D45P5313 2011   C843'.6   C2011-902216-8

Library of Congress: 2011930278

Cover design: Alysia Shewchuk • Cover photograph: Cosmo Condina/Getty Images
Text design and typesetting: Alysia Shewchuk

Canada Council   Conseil des Arts   ONTARIO ARTS COUNCIL
for the Arts   du Canada   CONSEIL DES ARTS DE L'ONTARIO

We acknowledge for their financial support of our publishing program the Canada Council
for the Arts, the Ontario Arts Council, and the Government of Canada through the Canada
Book Fund. We acknowledge the financial support of the Government of Canada through
the National Translation Program for Book Publishing, for our translation activities.

Printed and bound in Canada

For Nado and Kéli,
tender lands

To Martine Verguet,
for the sustaining words
— E. A.

For Izja Lederhendler, my brother, whose lifeline
traverses many boundaries in time and space.
— L. L.

And my father once said,
As he was praying on the stones:
Avert your eyes from the moon
Beware the sea, and journey not!

Mahmoud Darwish
"My Father"

ASKIA WOULD RECOUNT how in her final delirium, his mother had kept on about the letters that Sidi Ben Sylla Mohammed, his father, was supposed to have sent from Paris. Along with some photos. Which he had never seen. But then one day Askia went off on the same route as the absent one. He did not leave to find the missing father. He could live with gaps in his genealogy. He left because of a strange thing his mother had said: "For a long time we were on the road, my son. And wherever we went, people called us Dirty Feet. If you go away, you will understand. Why they called us Dirty Feet."

Paris. He was standing in front of 102, rue Auguste-Comte that afternoon because three days earlier, in his taxi, a passenger had intimated that she had once photographed Sidi Ben Sylla Mohammed. Scrutinizing his face in the rear-view mirror, she had said, "You remind me of someone. A man with a turban who posed for me a few years ago."

This was not the first time a passenger had used the you-remind-me-of-someone line on him, just to make conversation. Often enough an exchange of words would turn into a physical exchange, as an antidote to boredom. To the emptiness deep in the skin and the dark night. But that evening the girl had mentioned a turban, a detail echoing the distant words of Kadia Saran, Askia's mother. Yes, it was the same refrain: "You look like him, Askia," his mother had said. "Exactly like him. If you wore a turban, it would be almost as if he'd come back. Almost. Because he won't come back." He was an adolescent then. More than thirty years had passed. Askia had gone away, though not to confirm his resemblance to the absent father.

Still, he did want to see the photos, and the girl said that he could, but not right away. She would be away from the capital for one or two weeks, working on a project.

Askia's travels had begun because of another of Kadia Saran's mysterious pronouncements: "Our family is under a curse to depart again and again, to tramp over thousands of roads until we are exhausted or dead. Look at yourself, my son, endlessly wandering through the night in your taxi." It was hard to understand his mother and her words. All Askia knew was that his line of work obliged him to rove the streets. Yet in his flight across the pavements of the North he wanted to verify whether or not his machinery, programmed for roaming, could stop.

A dog and its mistress passed in front of him on the sidewalk. He recalled that as a child he would spend his days at the garbage dump in Trois-Collines, the squalid tropical suburb where he had landed with his mother. There he would mingle with dogs that he did not like. In particular the one belonging to old Lem. Its name was Pontos.

102, RUE AUGUSTE-COMTE. A newly refurbished four-storey building. Askia rang the doorbell. On the ground floor, to the left of the entrance, a window opened. He supposed this was the apartment of the concierge, someone — perhaps an old lady — banished to the desert island of this apartment, stationed there to challenge visitors with a thousand questions and drive away troublemakers. But it was not an old woman who greeted him. A man in his fifties thrust his head out.

"I have an appointment with Mademoiselle Olia," Askia said.

"The full name, please?"

"Olia."

"A given name doesn't tell me very much."

"She has brown hair."

"That doesn't tell me much either. Which floor does she live on? You have an appointment? I wasn't told anything. Sorry, I can't help you."

And the concierge shut his porthole. Askia lingered on the sidewalk. He was not angry. He simply thought this photographer, the passenger who had promised to show him portraits of his father, had had some fun at his expense. He headed across the street towards the Jardin du Luxembourg. The railings were hung with an exhibition. Pictures suspended in the sky of another world — still shots from a film: *Himalaya. L'enfance d'un chef.* Images from a far-off world, hung on the park fence. The large boards displayed people walking in various seasons. Like him. The wind hammered at his neck. He raised his coat collar and strolled several times around the fence and the pictures. The crowd began to thin out. The night engulfed the landscapes on display. The night overtook him. He decided to go home.

She came up behind him, surprising him in his dialogue with the faces on the boards. He followed her back across the street. She keyed in the code at the entrance to her building. They took the stairs opposite the door. The brass of the handrails and the sheen of the red carpet glimmered in the faint light of the hallway. They climbed the stairs, she in front and he at her heels. She stopped when they reached the top floor and slipped the key into the lock of the double door. He went in behind her.

The place was small, attractive, new. The front door opened onto a room that served as both living room and kitchenette. A sofa draped with an ash-coloured sheet faced the door. Behind the sofa was a bookcase with four shelves in the same white as the walls. He scanned the contents of the shelves: books, bibelots, an earthenware ashtray and bowl, a tiny square box made of wood.

Inserted among the books was a very broad bird feather that stirred with the slightest breath of air. The books lined the backs of the shelves while the bibelots were placed in front. On the wall around the shelves were some photos. He studied them. There was a noticeable connection among the faces on the wall. He had once leafed through a tome on the writers of the Harlem Renaissance and had no trouble identifying the four portraits arranged in a row high above the shelves: W. E. B. Du Bois, Alain Locke, Langston Hughes, Countee Cullen. To the right of the shelves, hanging one above the other, he recognized Claude McKay, Sterling Brown, James Baldwin. He was unable to put a name to the fourth face. The girl noticed his interest.

"I enjoy portraits of black people," she said. "They have a way of capturing and holding the light."

"My father has no connection with the celebrities on your wall. Could you show me the pictures you took of him? Wasn't that the reason you asked me to drop by?"

In front of the sofa, to the left of the front door, the TV and CD player sat on a large chiffonier. On the wall above the TV there was another photograph, which he found quite beautiful. It was the interior of a nightclub: a bar, high stools, two women and a man, all holding cigarettes between their fingers, their heads wreathed in smoke. The little group was standing around some musicians. He identified the elegantly dressed man at the piano as Duke Ellington, and leaning on the piano, cradling his trumpet, was Louis Armstrong. Askia had a mental image of his hostess attending the nightly concert given by Louis and the Duke. At the exact moment when the concert began, she would no doubt sit down on the sofa facing the picture to take in and savour the sounds emanating from the glossy paper on the wall. But his father, Sidi Ben Sylla, would not have moved in such circles. His music, Askia's mother would have said, was not jazz but exile.

Olia must have read his thoughts.

"You know," she said, "I sit down in front of

that picture and conjure up the concert, the notes. I imagine them soft and translucent and as slow as the water in a stream, at times lapping against the bank when the high notes soar into the air . . . Can we be less formal and call each other by our first names?"

"Musical notes — they can be sad too, miss. Now, about those pictures. Could you please show them to me?"

More photos lined the white walls, including the space in the far corner next to the TV, where some stairs led to a mezzanine and what Askia guessed was the bedroom. These other pictures showed Jesse Owens and the king, Carl Lewis, racing at full tilt, propelled by the gods of Olympus, and a very emotional Ella Fitzgerald at the microphone, with the beams of fame shining on her forehead. This girl Olia was peculiar. She evidently lived in a strange world filled with images and legendary figures. Askia thought she must be fond of legendary faces. She liked Owen and King Lewis, and Ella. But Sidi, the ghost he pursued through the dark Paris nights, was not a legend.

He plumped down on the sofa. She bustled about in the kitchenette, to the left of the shelves. She made some tea, set the cups, sugar, and teapot on the low table in front of her guest, and sat down on the floor in the lotus position. After the pictures

of the Himalayas, here was a second image of the
East for him to contemplate that evening: Olia sitting cross-legged as if to prepare for meditation, as
if he were an altar or the statue of a saint or an icon
meant for prayers.

"You really do look like the man in the turban I
photographed a few years ago," she said, laughing
with her eyes and dimpling the corners of her mouth
in a way that heightened her charm. Then she admitted that, following their encounter in his taxi, she
had searched through her photo albums for the man
with the turban. The portraits must have gotten mis-
placed in one of her many boxes. It would just take a
little time, but she would find them.

Askia had the impression that among all those
images on the wall, the only thing in the room that
was real was the shape of Olia's face, her hair tied in
a bun at the nape of her neck. She was neither too
short nor too tall. But thin. Her face had the original-
ity of a painting. Her body was ordinary. He thought
she should always wear black. Black — the depths of
night and mystery where her face had been drawn.
He discerned two small pears under her sweater.
Mother Nature could have been more generous, he
said to himself. But he felt that what was most striking about this person was not her appearance so
much as her personality.

The tea did him good. The tea and the warmth of this little home. And yet he was afraid. Afraid that the horrific hand bristling with razor-sharp hairs — the hand that lurked in his worst nightmares — might punch a gaping hole through the ceiling and seize him and cast him out of the apartment and into the cold. It was a dread that went back to his childhood.

Olia stood up, affording her guest a view of her outfit, black from head to toe. She crouched in front of the small fireplace built into the wall to the right of the door. She lifted the logs out from the ash, rearranged them, and lit the fire. The flames enveloped the logs, the soot-coated hearth began to glow, the flames rose higher.

3

THE FLAMES AND the question in the girl's eyes — "Who are you? Who are you?" — kindled a scattering of reluctant images in the haze of Askia's memories. The outlines of a village, a red dirt road travelled by herdsmen, back there, near Nioro du Sahel. The ground, heated by the rays of a relentless sun, rising towards the thick clouds in a fine dust that stuck to the skin. Nioro. As far back as his memory could take him, it was the point of departure. He must have been five or six years old. Nioro, or a dry patch of land somewhere in the vicinity. The long red road and a bridled donkey led by his father, Sidi, who had sat his only son, Askia, on the animal's back. Behind the donkey, the father and son, walked the mother,

Kadia Saran. On her head a basket of provisions, a bundle, a pouch holding vials with potions, amulets, and root sticks, a noria of remedies against all the ills of time — remedies to which only the herders of the great winds were privy.

All of them moved to the faltering tempo of the donkey, which could trot no faster than their flight over the sloping trails. Of this he was sure: it was there they had set off one opaque night steeped in a complicit silence. And when he hunted through his memory for the reason why they had departed, what emerged was the certainty that it could not have been in search of land for grazing. Because there had been no cattle left for a long while already. Only the donkey had remained, sole survivor of the epidemic that had mowed down their herd. This fact came back to him, and he saw their journey in a different light. A sombre light: the lack of rain in the Sahel, the burnt millet fields, the land covered with lizards through which despair crept in, the empty granaries, the stomachs hollowed out by hunger, and the gazes and prayers fixed on the horizon where the rain would come from.

He thought their departure had been because of that rain and the earth dying under their feet. He recalled those days spent crossing other arid lands, ravaged plains where a few souls hung on, resigned or reckless, full of hope or outright scorn. Scorn because the father, the mother, the son, and the donkey passing by their huts gave off a strange odour. The odour of many unwashed days. The mocking voices on the roadside:

"It's true we don't have any water left, but is that any reason to smell so bad?"

"Can it be that the wind's tongue may not have washed away their filth?"

"It's true that they are not to blame."

"They have no water."

"Still, is anyone entitled to stink like pariahs, like miscreants, like undesirables?"

"Can it be that the sand may have refused to scrub away their dirt?"

"Try to understand. The sand is hot. It's impossible to cleanse your body with . . ."

"Can it be . . ."

"That they . . ."

"Live on the long road . . ."

"Because the long road is all they have?"

Who are you? Askia read in the photographer's eyes and camera lens. This was how those few scattered episodes, the starting point of the roads he had forever taken, came back to him.

4

PARIS. A raw month of February running its monotonous course. His first meeting with the girl. He had forgotten to lock the doors of his taxi. She said, "You must have been sent by an angel — taxis are so rare at this time of night, especially on such a small street." And, without waiting for a response, she settled in and asked him to take her to Rue Auguste-Comte, by the Jardin du Luxembourg. Engrossed in the pictures she was deleting from her camera, she hardly looked at him. Their eyes met in the rear-view mirror, and he heard her explain, as if answering a question of his, that she used a digital for minor projects. She stared at him for a split second and returned to her business. She talked while selecting and deleting pictures. He followed her with his eyes, furtively spying on his customer as she purged her camera of portraits that did not please her. A bitter smile appeared on his face. Because it occurred to him in very precise terms that, four years earlier, before he had fled, he too had been wiping out faces with the click of a button.

He had taken boulevard Saint-Michel. There was nothing very complicated about this run. All he had to do was let his customer off farther along, near the Luxembourg gates. In front of the fountain bearing the same name as the boulevard: silhouettes gliding past, coats buttoned up against the dying winter, noises, moods, skins, a man standing alone with his back to a corner of the fountain, tending a grill and the chestnuts he sold to those scurrying over the cobblestones of Lutetia. The night had spilled its ink across the page of the day, the street had retrieved a light different from that of the old sun: signs glittering on the facades of the cafés, waffle shops, and newsstands. And another light streamed from the nimble fingers of a juggler, an artist throwing flaming torches, catching them and launching them back into orbit again. It was a beautiful performance, but he was afraid the juggler would get burned.

His passenger was still bent over her camera. He wanted to hear her voice again, perhaps assailing him with the music of her speech: *Isn't it a lovely night? Do you like chestnuts?* He wanted her to tell him something, a word, a thought: *You know, this technology makes things so easy. You can get rid of all the faces, I mean all the portraits, that aren't to your liking!* She raised her head, stared at him a second time in the rear-view mirror, and finally said, "You look like someone. But without the turban."

He shivered. What she saw in the mirror was not him. She saw someone else behind him, beyond his face. She lifted her head and introduced herself: "I'm Olia," and instantly went back to deleting pictures, the ones she found unsatisfactory, furiously hitting the buttons of her camera. They were caught in traffic near the Gibert Joseph bookstore. The passersby were rifling through the books laid out on tables on the sidewalk, searching for buried treasure, their attention focused on the volumes that they flipped through before dropping them back on the piles.

Askia was still stuck in the long line of cars with his passenger. In the meantime she lowered the window on her side and, leaning out her thin body, photographed the readers in profile.

5

FOR A LONG TIME he had sought to cleanse his mind of the memory of his father, that ghost, that stubborn shadow filling the film screen of his childhood, the screenlike wall at the foot of the bed where he slept in his mother's hut. It was 1973, and already three years had passed since the family had been reduced to the son and the mother huddled in their tropical shanty. The father was this: a film that started up at the end of a run, when he found himself alone in the car, images streaming down onto the windshield of Askia's taxi. In the film the father's faithful shadow loomed up on the wall in front of him at night in the hut. The father would play with a clown who sported a broad pair of wings on his back. Sidi, the father, who must have become associated with the clown at a travelling circus, wore a large white turban and inhabited the world of the dreamy child that Askia had been. Time had passed since their flight from the Sahel. The father and the clown did their routine:

Where are you going, big turban?

I don't know. I'm going.

You're going.

I'm going.

How far?

I don't know. As far as I can go.

You're going as far as you can go . . .

That's right.

And how far can you go?

If I knew, I would tell you.

You don't know where you're going. But you're going.

But I'm going.

And how long have you been going?

I don't remember.

If you knew, would you stop because you'd say to your-self: "I've been going for a long time and I don't know where, and I see this makes no sense?"

Probably. Because it makes no sense.

No sense . . .

But maybe you can try right now to stay where you are.

Where I am . . .

Paris.

6

HE HAD OFTEN wondered why Sidi had chosen Paris. He pondered this, searching for the logic behind this curious choice before recognizing the plain fact that he could find none. The logic eluded him, slipped through his fingers. Paris. It could have been a city on the Atlantic or Mediterranean coast, because in Askia's mind one of the reasons for leaving the Sahel had been to settle on the coast. Because the gods of the road had pushed them from the interior to the edge of those worlds. He thought that, logically, Sidi should have settled in San Pedro or somewhere higher, in Dakar or maybe Tangiers. It was hard to understand why Sidi had gone any farther.

What exactly had attracted his father to Paris? There was no answer to that question, yet he could still see how Sidi might have made his way to metropolitan France, *l'Hexagone*. When they had already made it to the coast — Askia was eight years old at the time — his mother would talk of those old tubs that frequently plied the route between the Gulf of Guinea and the shores of the Mediterranean. Once she had mentioned the men who sailed to Marseilles, having managed to hire themselves out on fishing boats whose captains were all too happy to employ such solid, brawny young men, able to winch up a net in no time, haul the big fish to the freezer for storage, and clean the small ones that were to be cooked for the crews. The men were sturdy and versatile too, veritable jacks-of-all-trades: cooks, mechanic's helpers, welders, maintenance men, and sometimes more. Sometimes lovers of sailors who found relief in their firm, smooth flesh.

Yes, Sidi may have reached Marseilles by following a predictable course, a logical itinerary from the ports of Lomé, Lagos, or Cotonou towards the south of France. And from Marseilles? Would he have then gone up to Paris? Or had he perhaps embarked in the Gulf of Guinea as a stowaway, only to be discovered far offshore and thrown overboard?

He reflected on the choice of Paris and he could see only that Sidi's case had probably not been so unusual. That from Cordoba to Bilbao, Matera, Rome, or Paris there were thousands of aliens tramping farther north. Some of them travelled great distances, towards Moscow, looking for knowledge in the university named after a Congolese political leader. There was one, Tété-Michel Kpomassie, who had gone even farther, towards Greenland and the lands of the Inuit, back in the seventies, his black feet sinking into the powdered snow up to the intangible limits of his curiosity while the compact people of the polar latitudes watched in amusement. And there were those too who did not go very far, their purpose being to earn enough money in the orchards of Sicily to feed their families, but there were those more frivolous, the sons of Berbers and Arabs, who invaded Andalusia from Tangiers as if to turn it back into Muslim territory as in the days of the Almoravids, when the suras were recited in the homes of Almeria.

Later, when Askia enrolled at the university in the eighties, he kept thinking about those different itineraries but never succeeded in placing Sidi somewhere, in a rural or an urban setting. Sidi evading all detection, pursuing who knew what mirage, driven by some obscure desire. His mother one day conjectured that Sidi had gone to France because he had a distant cousin from Guinea there. The cousin, Camara Laye, worked in a factory, which his mother believed was called Simca and was located in Auber- villiers, on the outskirts of Paris. In the early sev- enties, when Sidi had vanished, many people were migrating from black Africa and northern Africa to France, where they could work as labourers on con- struction sites or as employees in automobile plants. Yes, it was an acceptable explanation: in Aubervil- liers Sidi had met his cousin Camara Laye, who had assured him there would be a job waiting for him at the plant the morning after he arrived.

7

MORNING. Back in his apartment, a squat discovered with the help of Tony, an old schoolmate from the Université du Golfe de Guinée, his only contact in the French capital when he landed there on that cloudless early morning of May 2, 2005. When his friend had found him a place to stay he had said, "Thanks for the squat, Tony. This way I'll be ready to decamp on a moment's notice. Anyway, I'm not going to stay here too long. I'm indebted to you for the squat, my papers, and the contact for the taxi I'm driving."

His taxi licence was bogus too. But he needed those scraps of paper to be able to circulate according to the standards and dress code of the profession. To share in the Wedding. To belong to the world of those who move and make things happen. The appearances may have been false, but what mattered was that his quest was not, that at the end of the dark nights there would be the reality of his chasing after Sidi's shadow. For a few days he accompanied Tony, who worked as a deliveryman, on his runs through the city, thinking about his own route, the objective being not to deal out parcels and smiles to customers but to deal only with the road.

His room. Aside from the dampness of the green cracked walls, there was a grimy carpet pocked with a thousand landscapes. Holes. In the corner to the left as you came in there were pots and the hot plate, a tiny metal square with a heating element in the middle. Between the left corner and the right corner stood the radiator, which had never given off the slightest ray of heat. In the right corner was three-quarters of what had been a sink, where water still flowed, miraculously. The brass faucet poured out what he needed for cooking and drinking. And for shaving when he woke. On the wall above the sink hung a tiny blue cabinet. Opposite the kitchen utensils, the dead radiator, and the three-quarters of a sink was a mattress so ridiculously small for a man his size that he had had to extend it with his old valise, but even then his feet hung over the edge and threatened to punch a hole in the wall. His feet touched the wall, pressed against it, which was why Askia slept curled up on his side as if inside a belly. He was inside the cold, damp, dirty belly of an attic in Lutetia. Facing the front door, between the bed and the kitchen sink, was a window that overlooked his table, which consisted of a board placed on trestles that had been salvaged from the sidewalk.

He had a cramped view of the roofs, the chimneys, the stars. And of a skylight in the roof across the way, where he could make out the familiar muzzle of a dog that he did not like very much. A mutt that resembled the one belonging to Old Man Lem, which he would torture back then at the garbage dump in Trois-Collines. The dog, he recalled, was called Pontos, and he would pitch stones at it, together with his playmates, cruel children, at the most beautiful of all wedding celebrations.

8

HE REMEMBERED. The night his mother had made another of her strange pronouncements: "It must be a few months now that we have lived in this rotten district, my son. It must be a few seasons now since the muezzin's voice last resounded on our roof. Well, what you might call a roof. Months since we last prayed. We have always prayed in our family. But I see that nowhere here is there anything that could be called a mosque."

And the following day his mother had taken him through the rainy morning to the only Christian church in their shantytown. "The Prophet or Christ — what difference does it make to you, my son? One must still offer prayers to one or the other," she had said by way of justification. The church was a large shed. The rain clattering against the corrugated tin roof, the wooden corner posts overrun by termites so that, but for grace, the house of God could have collapsed at any moment without warning. The trellis walls breached by wide rectangular windows.

He remembered the animation of the throng of worshippers. The songs and the biblical text read by the pastor. Or the priest. What difference does it make? The text. Matthew 22:1–13: "The kingdom of heaven is like unto a certain king, which made a marriage for his son, And sent forth his servants to call them that were bidden to the wedding: and they would not come . . . So those servants went out into the highways, and gathered together all as many as they found, both bad and good: and the wedding was furnished with guests. And when the king came in to see the guests, he saw there a man which had not on a wedding garment: And he saith unto him, Friend, how camest thou in hither not having a wedding garment? And he was speechless. Then said the king to the servants, bind him hand and foot, and take him away, and cast him into outer darkness; there shall be weeping and gnashing of teeth."

Later he had asked his mother, "What's a wedding garment?"

"New, clean clothes."

"What's a wedding?"

"A celebration with new, clean clothes."

"And with people too?"

"With clean, nice-looking people in new, clean clothes."

"Will we be invited to the Wedding some day?"

"Possibly. But many people are never invited."

"Why?"

"Because of the clothes."

"And what happens to them when they aren't invited? They die?"

"Sometimes."

"Of what?"

"Of the cold. Or the sun. Of failure too."

9

THEY HAD ALL run aground on this square in the
middle of the city, like a derelict rotting in the port
of his childhood. Faces that Askia had met here, on
the plaza in front of the Centre Pompidou. Intract-
able. Immortal mugs. That's how he described them.
Adventurers, aimless runners, another incarnation
of failure. A few such disreputable profiles were loitering in the agora: Lim, the portraitist who had fled
Beijing in 1989; Kérim, with his slacker's muzzle, his
background, and the roads he'd travelled well hidden
inside his jacket; Big Joe from Marie-Galante, a muni-
cipal worker, in his green street-sweeper's uniform;
Camille the whore in her skirt slit a thousand times
on the front and sides, Camille swallowing bellyfuls

of Lutetian flesh, Venus of the crossroads of their
desires, her sex proffered to the city of a thousand
lanterns. He had been here long enough to get to
know them, having often come to stroll around this
place where, as Tony had informed him a short while
after his arrival in the capital, figures and shadows
came to mope from every pole of our old planet: the
pilgrims, the runaways, the curious, the unsatisfied,
all the souls fated to spin their wheels in the direction
of infinity. That is what brought him to the square —
the hope of bumping into Sidi in the infinity of his
flight, with or without the turban, which was surely
worn out from all the winds he had faced.

On the square were all the others as well, those
whom Askia did not know by name: the postcard
hawkers, the police officers, the high school kids,
the lonely grandmothers whose husbands rested in
Père-Lachaise.

There was the museum, all colour and metal; the
plaza, meeting place of the hour of exodus, filled with
peddlers, vendors of odds and ends, knick-knacks,
faces familiar or obscure, pretty little doll faces, girls
stepping through the doors of the museum and its
library at seven p.m., young ladies, their arms per-
ennially laden with heavy books. At seven p.m. the
heavy books spilled onto the pavement when they
crossed the threshold of the library, and they would

bend down to collect them. They squatted down as if for love, knees bent, and Askia could see their waists and the slenderness of their hips. Once a girl was holding a thick tome. It slipped out of her hands and lay unscathed on the square, and when Askia rushed to help her pick it up, he saw him. Sidi.

Sidi, serious and steely-eyed on the book cover, Sidi with a red cotton headdress coiled high over his tall forehead. The rest of the face sharply chiselled out of dry wood, straight nose, sweeping temples, supple bearded chin. Dry wood because the anxious face seemed impossible to soothe. Blurting out his question, he asked the girl where she had found this book with the portrait of a man he took for his father. She stared at him for a while, not understanding, before replying, "You mean the illustration on the cover? It's a portrait of Askia Mohammed, king of the Songhai Empire from 1492 to 1528. You think he resembles someone you know? Sorry, it's not who you think. Perhaps you are Songhai yourself? You have something in common with this picture? History is so fascinating, you know. It's part of us . . ."

Askia felt stupid standing frozen in front of the girl, who finally stepped into the museum on the heels of her delicate shadow.

10

SHE WAS A real pain in the neck. Olia. Askia had met up with her again. Two weeks later. In the same blind alley at Châtelet. Before he finally resolved to go to her apartment to see her. As usual, he was sleeping in the driver's seat with its back tilted down, waiting for dawn to bring a miserly night to a close. At dawn he could get the early birds. She tapped on the back door as she had the first time. And as he was barely emerging from the fog, she followed through: "Same as before. Rue Auguste-Comte." He understood. The drive was more relaxed this time around. It was late, Paris was asleep. She gave him her card again, thinking it necessary to add, "You may have lost the other one." He answered that he would come by her place to see the photos that she had mentioned the time before. The pictures of the man in the turban. Along the way he came to understand that she had a contract for a job at an apartment in the blind alley where he regularly stopped for a break. So it wasn't purely coincidental. In his mind he had nicknamed her the Blind-Alley Girl.

She was open. Like a road. Askia had stretched out on her sofa. With one arm bent behind his neck, he tried to read the book of the ceiling, as pale as the walls but lined with big wooden beams. He made a game of trying to guess how old they were, those beams extending horizontally above him. They did seem quite old, and possessed of a kind of coarse stylishness, the brown stripes of the wood on the white ceiling. They put him in mind of a ribboned sky, of roads running overhead and on which he drove an imaginary taxi. He quite liked the pattern of the beams, the white walls, the apartment of his blind-alley stranger.

She sat facing him in a lotus position. She probably did this often. A custom. Taking up this position in front of her guests. Her loosened hair somewhat altered her appearance. She looked younger. He sat up too. She wanted him to talk about his travels, to open the psalter of his wanderings. And the obvious thought once again occurred to him: *She is crazy.*

After all, he was a stranger in her house, and in the company of strangers it was best to be wary. It was a refrain he had often heard sitting behind the wheel of his cab. It set the beat of a city that was afraid. She urged him to open up.

"So, these travels of yours. Tell me. Because you, you're a battered ship lashed by the winds of many voyages."

"My taxi plunges into the dark streets. That is a voyage, a dark journey."

She did not understand. She insisted. "What are you talking about? The night is full of lamps. It's not dark."

"There are other nights. Which are dark. Which were. The past."

Still she did not understand. She said, "Yes, a few centuries ago this city was dark at night. The torches did a poor job of lighting the streets of Lutetia. But I find you mysterious. Obscure."

They drained their coffee without speaking and then she admitted she had not yet found the portraits of the man with the turban. Perhaps, she went on, it was not important anymore to find them. She could do his portrait, a new version of the man in the turban. Askia thought there was nothing to tell about his four years of futile searching in Paris. On the other hand, about his past . . . what he had become in the heart of the tropical night.

She went upstairs to her room to make a tele-
phone call. He focused his attention on the photos
hanging on the walls, which had spoken to him the
first time he had set foot in the apartment, the pictures of famous negroes. They lived on Olia's walls,
she who worshipped the time when the negroes of
the Sorbonne and the Collège de France were friends
of Jean-Paul Sartre, Robert Desnos, André Breton.
They had made a name for themselves in the Latin
Quarter, on the sidewalks there, in the cafés of Saint-
Germain-des-Prés. They had raised their glasses at
the Deux Magots, trading toasts with the light. Bantu
philosophy had flirted with Cartesian thought. He
flirted with Sidi, an image thinner than a thought, a
myth, a phantom father.

11

BEAUBOURG AND ITS square had become familiar to him. Its beautiful crowd as well. There were those going in and those leaving through the museum doors. Where a pair of guards kept watch. A few brave souls had set up their easels long enough to pass as portraitists and earn enough to warm their bellies.

The old man with a slight stoop had called out to him, "Good Lord! You haven't aged a single day! Though it's been a while. Thousands of seasons gone by and forgotten. Don't tell me you don't remember! Nigeria, 1969. You were walking on a country road. Biafra was not far away. You stopped my Jeep and asked me flat out, 'Do you sell weapons? I need one. To clear my reputation and regain my title as prince.' You do remember, don't you? You wanted to pay me with your ring. It was gold. And as if the gold were not enough, you unknotted your turban, where you'd concealed a few crumpled banknotes. Nigeria, 1969. No doubt about it! But what's scary is that you haven't aged at all! I apologize again. I had nothing to sell you that day. I didn't deal with individuals." This is what Petite-Guinée had said to Askia the first time on the museum square. His silver-headed, spare little body trembling with emotion. Askia too was shaken, but he had managed to say, "Biafra — that wasn't me." And it could not have been Sidi either. In 1969 he was still with his family. He hadn't yet disappeared.

Petite-Guinée was a mercenary. He had filled contracts in various places: Arabia, Sudan, Guinea, Uganda, Biafra, Angola. As far as Askia was concerned, those contracts were wars, faces, photographs of the distant territories where Petite-Guinée had plied his trade, an envelope in the folder of his memory. After packing it in, he had lived in Conakry. With a woman. She had died in jail there in the wake of a political conspiracy incident. That was during the mid-seventies. He said he bore that woman, that country, inside him like an unhealed wound. Hence the name Petite-Guinée. They became friends, and Askia would go visit him whenever he could to listen to old recordings of Bembeya Jazz from Conakry. And the old man would point out to him, "They don't make albums like that anymore! What do you say? That today's music is different? Even if the violence is about the same? And also the prayers for all of it to stop?"

Askia saw Petite-Guinée frequently. At night before starting his taxi shift. In the basement studio of the old man's bar in Montmartre. Over time he had become a painter. He wanted to map out on canvas all the roads he had travelled throughout his restless life as a mercenary.

Askia entered quietly. The old man confided to him that he had felt sick the whole bloody day, a fire scorching his soul, his insides smelling of something burnt. So he had taken out his box of brushes and colours, unfolded the easel that had been leaned up against the wall next to the frames, and tried to paint something. Anything, a scene, a figure, an emotion, his malaise. Carried along by the brush dancing on the canvas. He had painted a nighttime background, and within this preliminary void he wanted to draw the outlines of a concrete, palpable, sustained mass. Solid to the touch and the eyes. He wanted to reproduce the concreteness of a landscape or a human face, a pattern that would take over from the cracking, the shattering, the interior chaos he was experiencing.

He was a mess because he had never been able to untangle all the roads that he carried within. He wanted to see something linear and solid on the canvas: a stone house by the side of a perfectly straight road, a picture reflecting a standard existence, smooth and unbroken. The kind that Petite-Guinée would have wanted for himself. A life exactly like all the others. But for Askia it was the life of the mercenary, the pilgrim, the conqueror that was standard. An adventure like all the others in every respect. Since the Exodus, the Hegira, the Crusades, the yellow, white, or black gold rush. And all the invasions yet to come. The latest illegal alien, coming dirty-footed from the South to dig for bread-gold in Lampedusa, New York, Montreal.

Petite-Guinée swept his brush over the canvas. It scurried over the rough outlines, searching for shapes. He drew some haphazard lines but was soon disappointed. There emerged bits of architecture, demolished faces, shards, a stretch of road obstructed midway by a large black hole, debris, fragments of some unidentifiable ruin. In the loneliness of his nights, Petite-Guinée practised the art of exploding forms, destroying lives and roads. It could not be said that the colours on the canvas amounted to no more than an impression, an idea of failure, a concept, an elaboration. There was truth there. The debris on the canvas was necessary, like the remnants of a life or of a failure that spoke the truth. His own. The basic setting of his painting was a roadway littered with the shards and rubble of lives. He grew despondent and eventually dropped his brush.

Askia left without saying a word and went back to his cab. A calm night. The girls on Saint-Denis were shivering. No customers in sight.

He drove towards Boulevard Haussmann, Gare Saint-Lazare. Two blocks away, the flames of a fire. The air was burning. A scarf of smoke choked the globular moon, hanging from the edge of a gutter. He thought of a chapter from Revelation. Pictured the remains of lives that would drop onto the sidewalk in front of the blazing building. As in Petite-Guinée's painting. Pictured the remains of a body once big, bits of toes worn out from tramping over the pavement, a shred of cotton once an article of clothing, the turban shrouding Sidi Ben Sylla Mohammed's exile, his retreat. He pictured Sidi dead.

12

IN THE SHADOWS of Paris. His taxi crossed paths with fire engines. He prayed there would be a few skins left for them to save. Zero customers. He switched on the radio. The news report mentioned boatfuls of illegal African migrants grounded on the Canary Islands. Men and women come to find deliverance in Santa Cruz de Tenerife. Tomorrow he would turn on his radio again and there would be new boats, another story of flight, and the next day yet another chapter with people running away, and so on in the days, weeks, months to follow, until their feet gave out and the nomad sky ended.

At Les Invalides he picked up an old gentleman who had hailed him from under a lamppost he had been leaning against. The man wore an impeccable suit, spoke courteously, sprinkling his sentences with phrases such as *would you be so kind* and *forgive me* when explaining his destination. The man kept his eyes on him constantly. For a brief moment he seemed to hesitate, concentrating on the driver's face. Two bikers in leather jackets passed them before running the red light fifty metres away. *Life is short, brother, so why slow down?* A few seconds waiting at the traffic light. It turned green. Green, the go-ahead, and the man too went ahead:

"You know, I like skins."

". . ."

"I've been around the world and around skins. The flesh."

". . ."

"Kuala Lumpur, Phuket, Macao, São Paolo . . . They were young. The skins."

". . ."

"Please don't take this the wrong way, but yours reminds me of another. The face too. A head with a turban. It must have been a good ten years ago. He was standing in front of the Gare de l'Est and he was cold. Don't take this the wrong way."

". . ."

"A few years ago I experienced a moment of great intimacy with someone who resembles you. A

beautiful night. Serene and passionate. Quite a con-
tradiction, you might say. Don't take this badly, but it
was what's referred to as an encounter. Truly. Only,
his skin was dirty. But once he'd washed he was brand
new. Shining. Like you. But you won't take it the
wrong way, will you? A treasure of softness under the
filth. If I may be so bold, would you be interested?"

". . ."

"Please don't be upset. I could pay you the equiva-
lent of your night's earnings and a handsome com-
pensation on top of that. How does that strike you?
Of course, you could take a bath . . ."

". . ."

Askia dropped the man off in front of his mansion
and drove back into the night.

13

OLIA INVITED HIM over for lunch. She still had not found in her boxes the signs, the photos of Sidi Ben Sylla's passage through Paris. He started to tell himself, *Askia, it's all a joke. Sidi is a joke, the myth of a father you never had.* He had stopped as usual at the Jardin du Luxembourg. There were new pictures on the park fence. It broke the routine, this change of scenery in the city where he lived. He had often wished he could drive his taxi across the landscapes hanging on the fence.

This time the exhibition was about volcanoes. Beautiful shots. The work was titled "Of Volcanoes and Humans." Impressive, the orange summits with little yellow flecks, a music of lava descending a slope, the lava flowing, and standing there in front of the scene framed on the board, Askia thought, *The lava had better not descend too quickly. It had better cool before reaching the valley.* It must remain an image and not engulf the lane where he stood. The lane, the city, and Askia's quest. In the valleys where the lava was heaped, everything was grey. Roofs of ash on the houses and trees. The valley town inhabitants forced to leave. In long lines, bundles on their heads, their shoulders. He had not left because of volcanoes or lava. Instead it had been the murderous nights, the violence he had had to escape, even if, in that coastal city on the Gulf of Guinea devoted to torture, it was he, Askia, who had done the torturing.

Eventually he went up to Olia's apartment. She came very quickly to open the door, gazing at him intently, and he saw Modigliani's *Anna Zborowska.* He had seen the portrait in one of Petite-Guinée's art books. Olia wore a white collar like the woman in the painting and resembled her, but without the sadness or the long neck, like that of an Akagera giraffe. He called her Anna. In the painting, Madame Zborow-ska's first name could be discerned through the purple overlay of the background. Olia was surprised.

"Anna?" she said.

"Anna Zborowska. An invention. Listen, are you sure you didn't invent the man with the turban?

Those portraits you said you made, did you see them in a dream? What if the man and the portraits never really existed?"

"Does he matter to you, that man?"

"I don't know."

"You know, Zborowska, that sounds Bulgarian. Do you want to know where I come from? I'm from Sofia. That's what they call me, my colleagues at the magazine I work for. I take fashion photos, of models. I'm not crazy about fashion, but I have to make a living. I can't complain. It's well paid. I've been at it for ten years. The rest of the time I do things I enjoy. With my Leica."

They went out. She put her hand in his and confessed that she was famished. She took him to Le Bulgare, near Austerlitz. The train station. She wanted to give him a taste of Sofia, as she put it. The restaurant owner, who must have known her, gave them a warm welcome. He and Olia exchanged a few words in Bulgarian. She asked for the table in the back. They sat down. She ordered *shopska salata* as a starter because she had a craving for fresh vegetables. The main dish would be a pork *kavarma* with mushrooms and lots of onions. On the recommendation of their host, Askia chose *tarator* as his appetizer, a delicious cold soup made with yogurt and cucumbers. And for his main course, *pulneni chushki*, peppers stuffed with meat, tomatoes, and rice.

They ate with gusto. Askia focused his attention on the face of the girl sitting in front of him. She was hungry and savoured her *kavarma* with a lack of inhibition that pleased him. She did not hold back. She licked her fingers. She was not one of those high-society ladies with affected manners. She was Olia. Askia licked his fingers too. He felt good with this girl in the present tense of his story.

She confided that she wanted to go back. She missed her parents. It had been ten long years. Since she had seen her family, and Sofia. She had set aside enough money to provide for contingencies back home. She had finished building the house where she would live with her parents. In Sofia she would ask forgiveness of Saint Nedelya for having sold her body in the arenas of Lutetia. At first, in 1999. She had arrived in the city with a head full of plans and nothing in her pockets, having depleted all her savings to pay for the weeklong train ride from Sofia to Paris. A matter of survival. While waiting for word from one of the fashion magazines where she had left her CV, she applied for work as a waitress and a cleaning woman, but because of her vagabond gypsy appearance, the doors of the restaurants and homes stayed shut, so the only capital she could count on was her body. Until November 4, 2003, the day the owner of Le Bulgare, where she scrubbed pots and pans for fifty euros a week and a miserable maid's room in the nineteenth arrondissement, brought her a letter from *Orléanne*, a magazine interested in her work, in the pictures of anonymous models she had hired for a pittance in the narrow back streets of Sofia. Now all she wanted was to be back in her city, among her family and friends, in the haunts of her childhood. To stroll down the alleys of Borisova, to sit for a while on the front steps of St. Petka Samardshijska. Places that she carried inside her but whose shape she feared would in time be lost to her.

Askia, meanwhile, had no desire to return to his city on the gulf with the Fréau garden where dogs and men had been burned, the edge of the sea and the sadness of the rowers, the Place de l'Indépendance, where freedom had eventually been consumed by the flame held aloft by the statue in the square, the three murky lagoons that reeked of death, the lagoons where his father perhaps had drowned himself to cut short the long trek. So he should have asked himself, *What are you doing here, Askia? The father is an excuse. You made him up to account for your tribulations.* He had no wish to see the colonial palace and the ruined wharf again, the military camps that occupied the heart and belly of the city where he had grown up.

Olia had listened to him without interrupting, looking at him with an intent stare. He was unaware of how much time had passed. The waiter brought the bill. She wanted to go somewhere else. Askia took her to the Beaubourg plaza, where his friends went about their business.

14

ON THE WAY, he looked at the girl and sensed the question *Who are you?* coming back into her eyes. He thought that to say and to understand *Who he is* he would have to go very far into the past, to the curves and edges of those country roads that he had tramped over with his parents after leaving the Sahel. He would have to replay the scenes with the dead trees, the dry brushland, and the silence that had enveloped their migration. His mother would later inform him that it had been during the terrible Sahelian harmattan of 1967. Judging from his birth certificate, dated February 12, 1962, he must have been going on five years old, just as his scattered memories led him to believe.

During the family's migration, Askia had travelled a good portion of the way on the donkey's back,
but he recalled that his father would occasionally
lift him down from the animal, which had begun
to grow tired, probably from wondering where they
were headed. To which land's end they would march.
With the sparse grass under its hooves.

They camped by the side of the road during the
night, which was inhabited by the dream of that final
destination where they would at last be able to swing
open the doors of the house, tie the donkey to a tree
rising grandly in the middle of the yard, rest their
bodies, and begin again to make plans: find work, a
school for Askia, have more children, build friend-
ships, and hold celebrations — in a word, the ritual
of a life lived with a few joyful moments, and prayers
for those who believe.

He remembered that they were camping out
under the half-blind stars. In the towns and villages
they had passed through, the talk was about the mali-
cious pests that were devouring the fields. Migrating locusts. Or a similar species of small, voracious
chops. And in fact it was possible that their exodus
came about after the invasion of the locusts that
destroy everything in their path. Locusts, eating and
digesting the fields in an epiphany of utmost violence. And as they advanced along the red dirt road,

through the forsaken villages and razed savannahs, he saw that he was not the only one marching with his father, his mother, and the donkey. There were also the locusts that went ahead of them, trailblazers of the migration.

Who are you? he read into Olia's silences. And he thought of their journey. Of crossing through hamlets where the residents, standing in front of their homes, wondered, *Who are they?* The residents followed with their eyes the foursome made up of the father, the mother, the donkey, and the son, until they disappeared around the bend in the road. Among the residents, some took out machetes and slings to dissuade them from stealing even the most pitiful yam. These men and women scoffed.

"Who are they?"

"Who knows?"

"What I do know is that they're not from here."

"They're as long as the road they must have travelled."

"You mean that they don't resemble us; that they're thinner than us, we who've never gone down those long roads; that they're better-looking than us?"

"It's hard to disagree. They are better-looking than us."

"We're small and plain."

"Could it be that their bodies have grown sky-ward from always being on the march?"

"That they despise us from atop their sky-highness?"

"Yet can anyone deny that there is something noble in their appearance? Something princely, I mean."

"Princely? Now I've heard everything! So then, should we expect to see their court following behind?"

"It's easy to see they have no kingdom. Only the road."

"Is it possible they must spend their whole life on the road?"

"That they don't know the roads are not to be trusted?"

"One thing is for sure: they are dirty, and we can't let them into our homes."

And he thought of how best to answer Olia's question, *Who are you?*

15

A WEEK HAD passed. Askia ended his shift a little before dawn. He came back to his squat. His eight square metres of housing. A large cockroach came to join him on the mattress. It moved along his outstretched legs, starting from his toes, climbing towards his stomach before going back to circulate around his knees. For the roach, this journey, this itinerary mattered. It travelled on a road of skin, and Askia was surprised to be viewing himself as a territory. His cockroach's territory. After all, some meaning had to be ascribed to the roach's trek across his body. After all, the bug too needed a territory.

He got up. The cockroach disappeared down a hole where the walls met, gone to explore the corners of other rooms, other worlds. Askia stood in front of the sink. The brass faucet ran steadily, unflappably. An unstoppable leak. It had always leaked. Askia removed his coat and shirt. He took the towel from the cabinet above the sink. He wet it, rubbed himself down, then wrung it out, sending dirty water down the pipes. He repeated the procedure several times: wet the towel, wash, wring it out, wet it, rub the belly, chest, back, armpits, neck. To make up for not having been to the public bath in the Contrescarpe area. His pants flopped down alongside the coat on the mattress. He went through the same ritual again. He felt clean. A feeling that he could better see down into the depths of himself, with a hint of order, a modicum of clarity in his head. He pulled on his threadbare pajamas and lit the burner. The metal teapot heated up quickly. He immersed the teabags. Strong and sugared was how he took his tea. He put his sweater back on over his pajamas. In the window, the sky was a dark canvas.

Later someone knocked at the door. He opened. The man stood on the threshold of his room. Askia raised his eyes from the gumboots to the massive face. Black eyeglasses. He was easily six feet tall. Traces of dirt on his dark sweater. In his hands, an iron bar. His skull was shaven. Askia cleared his throat.

"What can I do for you, sir? Are you looking for someone?"

"I've come to help you."

"Help me?"

"To leave the country. You have to get out."

"I'm looking for someone."

"We don't like you hanging about here. It's a sanitation issue."

"Might I point out that there are stains on your sweater? It could be oil or ketchup or some other sauce, possibly some vomit as well. There's something vile about it."

"I've come to help you. You wouldn't want me to use my iron bar, would you? Isn't that right? You wouldn't want that, huh?"

"I'm looking for someone."

"Well, then, I guess he's not here. Maybe you'd have better luck in Zanzibar, Goma, or Lomé, huh? One of those towns in the ass of the world? You're not welcome here."

He woke up sweating. When he opened the window, the neighbour's dog was there across the way, immutable on the screen of the windowpane. Eventually he had started referring to him as Pontos, like Old Man Lem's dog. The one he and his buddies at the garbage dump in Trois-Collines had battered with iron bars one night because they wanted to spice up their games a little, because they had grown weary of stoning that hated mutt every day.

16

THREE DAYS LATER he parked in front of a dilapidated, deserted building. There were families living on every floor. He climbed the stairs to the last floor, the sixth, just behind Olia. There were no apartments up there. A large room, the walls covered with frescos, images of cities with colonnades, towers, walls rising out of clay earth. Depictions of battles: archers bending their bows, glittering blades cutting into a cloudless sky, blood-soaked savannahs. Street scenes as well: a crowd clustered around a kora player singing of a victory, no way of knowing which one. And below each picture was the name of a city or region: Timbuktu, Gao, Djenné, Oualata, Fouta-Toro, Dedri, Kano, Katsina, Zaria, Agadez. It was a beautiful mural, and even though there were a few dates providing some context — Cairo 1496, Mecca 1497, Agadez 1515, the Sahel 1516 — he would have liked to understand more.

The wind blew into the vast loft through the smashed shutters. The daylight heightened the colours of the frescos. Olia was calm. She scanned the room. Askia thought she had class, this girl from Opalchenska. Grace and tranquility. Opalchenska, the neighbourhood in Sofia where she had grown up. She told him that the man in the turban, Sidi Ben Sylla Mohammed, had lived here and had slept at the foot of the mural. It was here that Sidi had sat for her. That was ten years ago, a short time after she arrived in the city, when she was prowling around the recesses of Paris with her Leica, hunting for unusual images. The frescos, Sidi had said, recounted the story of the Songhai Empire and its king, Askia Mohammed. It showed the cities he had conquered and those he had passed through during his pilgrimage to Mecca in 1497. The man in the turban was not the one who had painted the mural. He had said, "No one knows who the artist was. But the main thing is that it exists."

Askia studied Olia's profile. Hard to say how old she was. But she couldn't be very young if indeed she had encountered Sidi ten years earlier. Her slenderness and the childlike quality of her face gave no

indication of her true age. She must have been thirty
or forty. Askia began to take her more seriously. With
her he was discovering a new chapter in the book of
Sidi.

17

BACK AT THE apartment at 102, rue Auguste-Comte, Askia wanted Olia to describe the photo session with the turban. If Sidi had in fact stepped in front of her lens and had actually agreed to stop for a while within the Leica's field of vision, he who was cursed with endless migration. The girl believed that Sidi had been willing to pose for her because he was not afraid that the lens would throw light on his soul and his many lives. And because he hoped the lens would fix him forever on paper and allow him to cast off the curse.

Askia returned later that afternoon. Her smile greeted him. They went directly upstairs to the mezzanine because she wanted to show it to him.

The wooden steps creaked under their weight. When they reached the top, there were two doors on the landing. She opened the one on the right, which led to a workshop-bedroom. It was actually another, smaller mezzanine built a metre and a half below the ceiling. A raised platform, Olia's bunk. Under the bunk, the floor. In the wall on the left-hand side was a closet that must have contained clothes and odds and ends, as well as books, some of which were scattered around the room. Boxes of film, lenses, pictures, or rather picture frames, arranged in a corner next to a spotlight mounted on a stand. And in the opposite corner stood a matching spotlight, as if in dialogue. Between them the walls were naked, empty, blank. There was a screen with a rather high barstool front and centre. Two mirrors, one oval, the other square, were positioned near the spotlight, alongside a large, rectangular table that occupied the whole partition opposite the platform. The table was covered with miscellaneous items: two crates, a ruler, pliers, a length of string, a lamp, thumbtacks, another box of film, a few gizmos that Askia could not identify, a bottle containing some brown liquid, and, at the far end, a teapot.

They drank the tea without speaking. Olia raised her eyes from the cup and squinted. She described how Sidi Ben Sylla had posed for her in front of the mural in the deserted loft. She had asked him to sit on a high stool against the background of colours, figures, words, and dates that told the history of the Songhai. He complied. She triggered the camera, shooting without a flash. She paused, pulled the spotlights from the corner of the room where she had placed them, and directed them at his face. It was harsh lighting. Sidi turned his head away. She told him to sit in profile, looking first in one direction and then the other, in full face, with his back to her, in profile again, first with his face lifted towards an invisible sky and then lowered towards a hypothetical river at the foot of the stool. Sidi was calm. Olia continued to shoot, capturing the immaculate strip of cloth above the broad forehead, the regular features of the face chiselled out of dry wood, the straight nose, the high temples, and the supple bearded chin. The clicks of the Leica pelted down on Sidi's turban.

Following the session, her strange model appeared sad. He let out a sigh before continuing. "You know, I've been on the move so much I've lost a few addresses. If I had them I would ask you to send a photo to my uncle Sidi Barouck in Nouadhibou, another to my brother Saidou, who stayed behind in Zinder, and finally one to my old aunt, who has probably passed away, in Médine, near Kayes."

"I'm very sorry, Sidi."

For Olia it was impossible to forget Sidi's gestures and words that day, even though ten years had gone by. His voice still resonated in her head.

18

THEY WENT BACK down to the living room and Olia became very serious. She took up her usual lotus position in front of the low table, on which they had set their cups of tea. "The man with the turban," she said, "stirred up something inside of me. An emotion that brought another one back to me. The past."

The past. Harlem. A trip, an encounter, a man who had been a passage in her life. But Askia did not understand right away.

"Harlem . . . a man, a friend, a one-time lover? Someone you loved?"

"Harlem, America."

Harlem was where she had taken her first pictures. The first real ones. She had completed her training in photography in Sofia. But without much enthusiasm. The passion — true, pure, jolting — would come later. In Harlem. Her first trip. She had been invited there by Penny, an American woman whose education in photography had followed the same path as Olia's and who wrote in her letters how the soul of Harlem inspired her. Nothing had inspired Olia up to that point. So it occurred to her that she needed her share of voyaging, a pilgrimage to the Mecca of what for her could be new and different. She might have gone to Bombay had she known someone there. To Lima, Recife . . . She went to Harlem because that was where her friend Penny was.

She told Askia that it was there that everything had started. Thanks to Willy, an artist doomed to freeze to death on 125th Street. Willy photographed the feet of passersby. He said he was capturing the feet, fixing on paper feet that could never stop walking.

She made a point of exploring the neighbourhood on her own. That bothered Penny, but it also gave her time to concentrate on her own projects. Olia found herself in the vicinity of West 144th, near the Studio Museum, where, Penny had said, certain artists were in the habit of storing their material and their dreams of greatness. She met Willy there, one fall afternoon in 1996 with the leaves painting the landscape yellow and the incipient frost tickling their toes.

She had her Leica. She strolled and took photos of an old crone stooped over her cane as she walked her dog; a grocer who resembled the Brazilian actor Grande Otelo, smoking a pipe in front of his store; a child who must have had the day off from school, bouncing a ball. In front of the Abyssinian Baptist Church, a pastor sermonizing with a stack of Bibles beside him.

This was Harlem more or less as she had imagined it. But she wanted to see more. She was contemplating a visit to the Studio Museum when she saw him. Willy. On the sidewalk in front of the museum, he shouted unabashedly:

"If you were an angel you would pose for me, beautiful! If you were an angel you would say yes like an angel who never says no! If you're agreeable, I'll take your portrait and your feet. Please, don't turn down the most famous photographer on 125th Street. If truth be told, I'm honouring you!"

"I'm not an angel. Just a tourist."

She found him funny, entertaining. She agreed to pose for him if he showed her around the museum first. He could help her. Help her to locate the soul of this place that he knew so well. They passed under the large glass marquee overhanging the museum entrance and pushed open the doors. He explained the history of the institution since 1967, the famous exhibitions that had been held there, and the one he hoped would someday be devoted to his work. And then for three whole days he showed her the places — cafés, bars, squares, lanes — all the subtleties that are apt to elude the sightseer's hurried eye. And for three whole days she posed for him. Jokingly, he said he wanted to photograph her in three dimensions: full-face to catch the light of her being, in profile to capture the intimate part of her, from behind to imprint on film what he called her mystery. She played along, and on the third day he brought her the negatives. In three dimensions: her being, her profile, her mystery.

After that he went on to her feet, which he took in the act of walking. Because, he said, they were a story. What's more, they were beautiful. Olia's feet. They barely touched the ground when she walked. She didn't want to take root. She was unable to. She was not of that breed. Willy said all these things to her.

It was a splendid adventure but there was something amiss. The little cough nagging at Willy when they first met had worsened. It had been cold the past two nights in the alley that was home to a few unfortunates, including him. He told her that all America had given him was the alley where he slept at night and a red and blue sleeping bag with a star over his heart when he lay on his back rather than on his side, as was his custom. The alley, the sleeping bag, the star, and a birth certificate: William Locke, born June 27, 1959, in Montgomery. From Alabama he had trekked up to New York on foot. He coughed, but he was proud and happy because his portraits of Olia's feet were good, and this made his small, shrivelled body quiver with emotion. There was fire in his eyes. Not the sort that warms the insides but the violent kind that burns and consumes a person. Willy was consuming himself. He wanted to give her the pictures but she refused. She tried to convince him they were good enough to draw a connoisseur's attention, and who knows? But he coughed even harder and wanted to sit down on the curb and catch his breath.

He ended up lying on his side, with both hands pressed against his heart. In a final effort, his left hand slid down to his jacket pocket, pulled out the negatives of his latest work, and held them out to her. She looked around for help, spotted a phone booth at the far end of the block, and ran over to call 911. When she came back, he greeted her:

"Delighted to have made your acquaintance, beautiful. You have superb feet. Looks like you were lucky enough to have met the greatest artist on 125th Street before he left to join the gods. Looks like his time has come. You know, I hope that in Hell they stop going up from the South to the North to find salvation. I hope that, down there, we can finally come to rest . . . It's still a great mystery. The title I gave your portraits is 'Olia and Her Feet' . . . Olia in . . . my . . . Goodbye, Olia."

"Goodbye, Willy."

She was disconsolate. The firemen arrived twenty minutes later. Willy had died speaking of "Olia and Her Feet." When she returned to Sofia, she developed her friend's last pictures. The luminous shadows of the negatives proved to be a poignant study of the vast metropolis's hurried steps. Walkers. An exploration of how far the steps could go, of how many times they could be multiplied.

Feet can get tired too. But is that visible in photographs? When they are printed, can one step be told apart from the next? The step that is coming from the one going away? The step that knows where here is from the one that does not?

19

ASKIA WAS MOVED by Willy's story. And, as sometimes occurred in such cases, he spent a troubled
night dreaming of Sidi. He found himself in the
countryside. Sidi was taking him to the bank of a
creek that cut through a wood. He liked Sidi's smell,
a mixture of incense and cowpats. It came from his
grimy hair, the haircut that lent him the appearance
of a Rastafarian in some Kingston ghetto. He was
not wearing his turban. They sat down on the grassy
bank, and Sidi spoke to him, proud to open the book
of his speech. He told him a strange story, the story of
Juan Preciado, a young man searching for someone
who was absent, his father, in the ruins and shadows
of a village named Comala.

The young man in Sidi's book wandered the roads, questioning living beings who turned out to be anguished ghosts, fleeting forms with peculiar names: Pedro Paramo-Ulysses, Doloritas-Eurydice, Susana-Electra. These names meant nothing to the child he was in the dream. Yet he liked the aura of strangeness that enveloped them, the mystery that they inhabited, and Sidi remarked that the ghosts came from a great mythology: their names, their destinies, the location of the villages, the roads they haunted. They were men and women on the move.

Most of the story escaped him, but he urged Sidi to go on with it. He needed to know if the young man from Comala finally discovered signs of the absent one's passage. He thought the phantoms might have informed the young man. But Sidi cut him off: "End of story. I'll tell you the rest tomorrow. Just keep in mind that Juan Preciado is still searching for the absent one, Pedro Paramo, according to the official records. Remember that he follows him, walking, running, riding a sorrel mare, a train, a bus, a taxi, in the hope of finding him as quickly as possible."

"The young man in the book," Sidi explained to him another day, "is Telemac. A nice name, don't you think? Wouldn't you like to have it? I'll gladly give it to you . . . Take the name and forget everything else — the roads and the search that will wear you out."

His waking cut short the troubled night.

20

OLIA'S MEMORIES WERE the only evidence that Sidi had come through Paris. She did not see him again after their photo session in the loft. Her strange model seemed to have been sucked into the frescos showing the ancient cities of West Africa. He had entered into the world of the characters in the mural.

Askia went back to his cab, his runs. An old woman got in at the Madeleine. Shivering all over from the cold. Crumpled by the seasons and the years. She settled into her seat and he sensed that she was uneasy. She scrutinized the interior of the car, tested the seat, brushed her small, trembling hand over it. She finally told him where she wanted to go. After making the first turn he felt that she was still uneasy.

Two minutes later she asked if he was from Onitsha, in Nigeria. When he did not answer immediately, she continued. "I've just returned from Onitsha. A photograph of a man who resembles you is going around there. He wears a turban. They say he is a taxi driver. Underneath the photo it says, 'Do not get into a taxi driven by this man.' The man is rumoured to be a ghost who picks people up to kill them in the seedy neighbourhoods on the outskirts of Onitsha. Uh, you're not that man, are you?"

"..."

"Apparently he does no favours to the people who get into his taxi. He kills them. I was lucky — I didn't come across him. Actually, I didn't leave the hotel very often. Didn't mix much with the local population. That's what you have to do — not mix. Are you from Onitsha?"

"..."

"It seems that, despite the turban, the man is a voodoo priest. He offers up his clients as sacrifices. Cuts their throats! They say he is insane and bears a curse that he can't get rid of. The curse is that he can't keep from moving. He was condemned by some gods, Shango and Oya Igbalé, I think. That's what they say in Onitsha. Sentenced by the gods to travel forever. So to put an end to the curse he must sacrifice people! Well, at least he doesn't act that way out of wickedness. It's because of the curse. Listen, you wouldn't be that man?"

"..."

"Apparently he murders them in the basement of his house, which is full of sanctuaries, little nooks filled with the presence of spirits, altars with statuettes, massive rough terracotta busts, Legba statues, which I was told he'd had sent from Ouidah. It's said the man pours his victims' blood on the Legbas, the pyramid-shaped altar, the white of his boubou. Hey? You aren't from Nigeria, are you? You're not that man?"

"..."

"I suppose the malediction has not ended, because he can't keep from slitting the throats of those poor people. He runs around making one sacrifice after another because he wants to stop running ... Hey, are you a real taxi driver? You don't do these runs because you want to stop running? You're not him? You haven't changed cities?"

"..."

"This is where I get off, sir. Keep the change!"

The old, frightened woman got out and scuttled down the sidewalk, back in the direction they had come from.

21

ONE DAY — he must have been barely an adolescent at the time — his mother sighed. "My son, I'm afraid you won't be able to elude the curse. It's enough to see how you scan the horizon, how your eyes search beyond the boundary of the earth and the screen of the clouds. I sense that you too will leave, Askia; I always knew it. My prayers have served no purpose except to open the roads even wider . . ." She was sad right then. They were living in the shabby little town on the outskirts of the big city where they had landed after their exodus. His mother said that his father had stayed on the road. This was necessary, she assured him. Askia had to be shielded from the father's baleful presence and aura.

During all the years they lived in that shabby town she was a cleaning woman for people who lived in the real city, on the plateau. Because she had sent him to school and that cost money. And when he came home after school, he recited his history and geography lessons to her. There was that afternoon when the class had been about Timbuktu. The teacher, Monsieur Christophe, spoke of a city where for five centuries thousands of travellers had converged. Timbuktu, somewhere in Mali, the same territory where Nioro du Sahel was situated. The city from which they had departed twelve years earlier. The teacher cited the names of the travellers who had trod the sands of Timbuktu: Ibn Battūta of Tangiers, Leon the African, René Caillé, and many others who had come from lands beyond the dunes of the mysterious city. Askia thought that Sidi had gone back there. In Timbuktu Sidi had found peace and practised many trades. He was a merchant, a basket maker, a weaver, a sculptor, a magician, a storyteller, a gold dealer, a camel breeder, a poet, and an architect working on the blueprints of the house where he would live after his long journey.

History and geography were more than a passion for Askia. These subjects offered him the possibility of finding refuge in unknown worlds. He wanted to succeed and earn enough money to take his

mother to the faraway cities that his teachers alluded to: (Lourdes, Marie-Galante, Syracuse, Capri . . .)
He would take the old globe that his mother had salvaged from one of her employers in the real city, and pick a city, any city, by randomly placing his finger on the globe. The map of the world would spin on the rusted trunk that served as a table and his finger fell on different cities: Mexico City, Jaipur, Saint-Louis du Sénégal, Florence, Beirut . . .
His finger on the elsewheres in which his mother could start her life over with a man who would stay put, stuck to the earth and the bodies of his loved ones.

The globe spun and his mother yelled:

"Stop that game, Askia! What good does it do to wake the gods of the curse?"

". . ."

"You mustn't, my son. They might rouse from their light sleep and send us back on the road! Don't you like this city?"

". . ."

She gripped his shoulders and squeezed them with a fever in her eyes. This frightened him and he changed his plans. He grew more careful to avoid waking the gods of the road. He did not want to leave anymore; he organized his life around the shacks of the slum while in his dreams he saw Sidi running across the old globe, alone, in the middle of a city-scape with high towers and dense traffic.

He abandoned his plan of freeing his mother from the seedy neighbourhoods. So it was a great surprise to hear her say one morning as she shook out their sheets, striking them against the trunk of a dead acacia in front of their shack: "This country isn't worth a penny. It's not worth staying here. You must leave, my son, my knight. Your dreams must take you beyond the threshold of our hovel."

In the early eighties, when he found himself studying anthropology and literature at the Université du Golfe de Guinée, he discovered Cervantes' *Don Quixote*, one of the knights-errant, who are described as those who live their dreams and dream their lives. He was struck by the similarity between the description and what his mother had said, she who had never read anything but the book of her misfortune. Three years later, having just finished his degree, he was recruited by the Cell. He had become an anti-knight, a dark knight, a midnight wolf at the wheel of his taxi, moving in for the kill.

22

A DULL DAY. Askia was beginning to grow bored after four years of wandering through Paris with nothing to show for it. Or could it be the weight of his forty-seven summers already pressing down on his broad, slightly stooped shoulders?

Olia greeted him with these words: "It's not worth it anymore, Askia. It's over — the time for acting the part of some obscure, obsessed Telemachus." Her eyes shone. Askia expected her to add something else that might enlighten him. The apartment smelled of repose, the wood burning in the fireplace, an aroma of the story's end, when people come back to the hearth to warm their limbs frozen stiff with adversity. She had put on an album, Duke

Ellington's *Take the "A" Train*. He understood this music — there would be other trains left for him to take. And yet he could not quite grasp the significance of the girl's words.

So she said, "I've found the man with the turban. He's returned to the top floor of the building where the Songhai frescos are. He's back in the picture. What do you say to that? Say something!"

Askia remained curiously silent. Sidi, he thought, was playing a game, hiding or showing himself on a whim, erasing and restoring his footprints in the sand of the cities.

Olia shook his shoulder. "I'm taking you to the loft."

" . . ."

She took his hand in the street. They went down into the metro. His cab was in the garage because of a breakdown. The mechanic had announced that it would easily take half a day to get it running again. Until then he could take a break.

Olia was a little restless. Eager to see the turban again. He felt nothing. At the Châtelet station she let go of his hand and left him behind, walking ahead of him on the metal carpet of the moving sidewalk, the treadmill. She ran and stopped in the middle of the long grey belt conveying them to the way out. He saw her from a distance on the stage of the treadmill, her delicate feet on the metal. Olia standing there with her tinted hair and long skirt, the girl from Sofia on the stage of the moving sidewalk in the belly of Lutetia, planted on the music of her feet, turned away from the direction the metallic ribbon was moving in, turning her back to the world on the move but facing the other riders on the treadmill. With her long skirt she could well have been assuming the preparatory position, the genesis of the first steps of a Russian or Zulu ballet, Olia onstage somewhere in Kamchatka or Bulawayo, ready to perform the first dance in celebration of the end of all quests and the exhaustion of the roads.

The strips of the steel belt slipped by under her feet and were swallowed up under the smooth surface of the cement that came after the treadmill. Askia saw her on the last strips just before they reached that smooth surface and was afraid she would go under with them. He leapt forward, jostling an old woman who was in the way, and grabbed Olia before she was devoured. He lifted her, and, propelled by the final thrust of the belt, they ended up on the ground, with Askia's bulk enveloping, covering, cushioning the fall of Olia's transparent, slight, fragile body. They laughed like children, to the applause of an indigent who looked like a Negus — a shock of hair and a serene face — sitting in a corner and reeking of urine.

A man with the cup and drama of his misery placed at his feet. On his chest the Negus of the metro carried a rectangular piece of cardboard bearing a message: *A coin and I bless and cover your flight.* Askia approached the man while rummaging in his pockets. The man chortled. His chin danced and displayed the ruined landscape of his teeth, the landscape of his gladness at trading a smile with the world.

They hurried towards the turnstiles. Olia hoisted her leg over the horizontal bar blocking the narrow passageway and slipped her small body through the tiny space between the ground and the gate that swung open to let commuters through. Askia was taken aback. She had retained something of the rebel, the outlaw. He searched in the pockets of his jacket and eventually pulled out a folded ticket that he inserted in the slot of the machine, but it would not let him pass. The horizontal bar refused to yield to the pressure of his legs and the small electronic screen flashed red: *Ticket not valid!* He repeated the procedure. *Ticket not valid!* Pushed the bar. *Ticket not valid!* Back in his corner the Negus giggled and said, "I see you're not valid. You don't have the right ticket to get through the gates of Lutetia. You're not valid! You don't have the right ticket to go to the ball on the other side of the barrier!" Then the Negus handed him a ticket and Askia passed through the turnstile and joined Olia, who was waiting for him with a teasing smile. She was being somewhat derisive because she had believed that he, the rhapsode, could open any door in the world.

He started imagining that Sidi had returned to Paris. He pictured his sire in the metro, pushing a shopping cart filled with his belongings and food, some stew from the food bank where he had made a stop. People were bothered by the smell, turned heads in his direction, then uttered obscenities, but some smiled too because he was funny, this man in the metro pushing a shopping cart filled with his belongings and some stew. They scrutinized his long silhouette from the immaculate turban to the oddly clean bare feet. Askia could not say why he imagined Sidi barefoot. Then he saw him on the street, walking towards his loft, the land of the frescos.

They went down ten steps to the platform. Their train would be there in about ten minutes. Askia thought back to his city on the shores of the Atlantic, a station where trains no longer stopped because there were no tracks left. On the board bolted to the concrete wall above their heads, illuminated letters and numbers indicated the stations remaining before their stop: Luxembourg, Port-Royal, Denfert-Rochereau. Seeing the series of names, Olia was thinking out loud of another series, her metro line, the stations she went through before getting off at Opalchenska: Vardar, Konstantin, Velichkov. So Askia in turn was prompted to silently perform the same mental gymnastics. He saw in a flash the green minibuses of his coastal city, the bus ride that invariably cost fifty francs, the ride to Kodjoviakopé, which first had to go through Bè, Amoutivé, Hanoukopé, Nyékonakpoé . . .

The train finally arrived amid the plaintive tune of its brakes. They chose car number seven because Olia was superstitious. She believed that nothing could happen to her in car number seven, that no evil spirit would slow their ride in car number seven, because the music had whispered to her, *Take car number seven, Olia* . . . She was reassured. She was not afraid.

23

THEY WERE FRIGHTENED when they came out on the sidewalk in front of the old building. Horrified by the apocalyptic scene of flames licking at the windows, making the panes explode and crash in splinters on . the asphalt below with the sound of tolling bells, tolling for the bodies inside the building, bodies letting out earth- and soul-shattering cries, bodies falling together with the glass onto the cold asphalt.

The fire had broken out on the ground floor. From there it climbed to the upper floors, engulfing, scorching, charring the damp, porous, cracked walls. Driven by a merciless wind, it seared the walls and the people. No part of the building was spared. The whole thing was ablaze. They stood rooted before

the reddening structure, the dead windowpanes at
their feet. Wailing. Moaning. The last signs of life,
of a clinging to hope. On the ledge of an overheated
window, a pair of feet testing the void for a place to
stand. But the void was powerless and had nothing to
offer the feet but its inability to bear them. The hands
gripping the window frame let go, and that was all.
Askia started for the front door of the building. Olia
grabbed his sleeve and held him back. It would do
no good, she said, the cries could hardly be heard
anymore, and what that meant was obvious. Besides,
sirens were approaching and the red of the fire trucks.
The firefighters of Lutetia coming to the rescue of the
poor creatures trapped in the ruins of the smoking
tomb. Olia shouted that the firemen were going to
collect the remains and harvest the writing of the
dead, the burnt letters on the wall.

The smell of burning was the same — O horrific childhood! — as what he and his confederates
had smelled that time at the garbage dump in Trois-
Collines when they had tried to burn Pontos, Father
Lem's dog. Rigo, the cruellest among them, had gone
to steal some gasoline at the Texaco station in the
business district. After that they had only to wait,
because they knew that Pontos would come as usual
to get his scraps at the dump, the maternal provider
for all of them. And so, before the onset of twilight

heavy with the stench of rotting garbage, the dog appeared, muzzle twitching, tail held low. The children fell upon him. With a strength born of despair he freed himself, but they managed to burn his tail. O Pontos, why did those kids hate you so?

24

THE BUILDING WAS burning. In the hearth of the night Olia stood frozen. Perhaps she too was dead, a charcoal statue unable to grasp what was happening, an unhappy piece of work created by that cynical artist, fire. Whose ends were murder and ashes everywhere. In the end, death and ashes. The firemen who eventually came found the end result, and blamed it on the gas raging through the slit throats of the old building's pipes.

Askia saw the sequence of events. The events previous to their arrival on the scene. Sidi lying on the floor beneath the frescos. Before the shock of the fire he had gotten up to look out through the smashed shutters of the loft at the grey facade of the building across the way, a lighted window framing a woman in black who was savouring the pleasure of at last witnessing the apocalypse she had so desired, her feverish eyes riveted on the loft. And below, in the silence of the street, the dark metal ring of a gas outlet where a doddering old man had stopped to warm himself, holding his shopping bags and a doubtful treasure just salvaged from the green garbage bins of the building across the street. He was thinking of the generosity of the trash bins of Lutetia. As green as hope.

The window. When the fire broke out, that was where Sidi was going to escape. Jumping into empty space. But he wanted to take the shopping cart with his belongings, his souvenirs, and some leftover stew. He made an about-face. Stepping in the direction of the cart, he bumped up against a greasy box that was lying there. He fell and struck his head against one of the pillars of the loft. He blacked out, and when he regained consciousness, it was too late. The windows were hung with curtains of flames, the staircase was a furnace. He watched the fire consume the columns, the walls, and the towers painted on the cement. The fire seized hold of the clay fields, the yellow savannah, the horrified people in the frescos, the heart of the cities: Oualata, Kano, Katsina, Zaria, Agadez . . . the skirt of his robe and the mementos in the cart: a photograph, some earth in a small bag, a few coins, a worn-out pair of shoes.

25

MOMENTS OF GLOOM. The strollers on the banks of
the Seine were few. Because of the weather. An icy
sky. Olia was away, delivering an order to a client
who was in a hurry. The start of another day. Askia
raised the collar on his jacket. He noticed that there
were more creases on the surface of the water. A
bateau-mouche was approaching. After it had slipped
by, a good half-hour elapsed before the water could
once again stretch out, a smooth, ironed, tranquil
bed. Very soon the wrinkles returned. A police boat
patrolling the banks. Because there might be someone careless, or suspicious, a *sans-papiers* who might
not be entitled to that spot on the riverbank where
he sat freezing, hands quivering, lips too, coughing,

hugging his jacket tight to his chest. Askia tried to stand up. How long had he been there motionless, a useless feature in a setting where, on the contrary, everything — people, events — was supposed to move?

Eventually he got to his feet.

He retrieved his taxi at the garage and drove down to the parking lot. He did not have the slightest wish to go back to his squat. Which looked like the building that had burned, a damned rest stop where he had paused to catch his breath. But a place to stop was a trap for people like him. You plant your butt on a riverbank, have a drink, rent a motel room, take a liking to a girl you've met by chance, and before you know it the sky crashes down and consumes you and your vessel, which was only searching for a harbour and about to moor in the belly of that one-night lover. Of this Sidi had surely been aware. He had gone back to die in the trap of that old rest-stop building. Otherwise he would have pushed his shopping cart farther, towards other passages, other landings.

Olia had said that she had seen the man in the turban again, on the train. He had not recognized her. It was on the number four metro line, which runs from Porte d'Orléans to Porte de Clignancourt, the underground thread between the south and the north of the city. He was travelling from the south of the city northward — that was his life: to leave the South of his childhood and trek towards the North of his wanderings. She had followed him.

Askia believed that if he returned to his ghost building, his squat, he would burn and cause others to suffer. He therefore decided to live from now on in the shifting space of his taxicab. He climbed into the driver's seat and tilted it back. He preferred not to lie down in the back seat as some of his colleagues did. He had the feeling that if he did he would be taken somewhere. Naturally. That was the seat meant for passengers, who were to be taken somewhere . . . The past. The Cell.

He lay on his back. An atrocious pain shot up his spine. He turned on his side. His body felt heavy. He experienced something resembling sleep, a weight that pressed down on his eyelids in spite of his discomfort. He was propelled into another sky, another universe, a reality with a door opening onto a streetless city.

26

HE HAD ON occasion amused himself by imagining the contours of the streetless city. The contours because, if this city existed, obviously nothing but its contours could be imagined, since it had no streets. It would be a great mass of bricks or concrete where all things would be enclosed: people, animals, objects, projects, plants, all shut inside the grey mass, cloistered in cells for all eternity without any possible view of the outside. The great mass of the streetless city would contain everything — shops, public squares, bars, libraries, churches of every denomination, *filles de joie*, monks, hospitals, cemeteries — everything except a view of the outside and, perhaps, a street through which the inhabitants of the streetless city might escape and spread out over unknown and at times dangerous roads. In his dreams he sometimes lived in the streetless city.

He often went to see Petite-Guinée on nights when he was feeling low. He enjoyed finding himself in this bar, with its decor of hazy nights warmed by the soft light of the lampshades and the barman's unchanging, practised gestures: serving, refilling, clearing away the glasses, rinsing his hands, placing them on the counter, offering a smile to a new customer who had adjusted his itinerary to include the bar.

The barman smiled at him. "What's your pleasure, Askia?"

"Whatever."

"Which, if I'm not mistaken, means whisky?"

Askia stared at the glass, then drained it in one go. His fingers strolled over the varnished wood of the bar. He tapped on the smooth surface. There was some Miles Davis playing. The notes drifted up from behind the bar. Miles's "Bye Bye, Blackbird" rose like a joyful, translucent requiem.

Petite-Guinée arrived — his small, unobtrusive body, the slowness of his movements, the wrinkles in his smiling face. Askia realized that he had no more than an abstract, fragmentary idea of the book of his friend's life: Born in Montmartre, a happy childhood spent in a choirboy's surplice serving Mass at the

Sacré-Coeur, an unhappy adolescence spent with the shame of having a *collabo* as a father, his youth spent as a roving seaman trailing his quest through the ports of old Europe. Adulthood brought him a career as a mercenary, the love of his life dead in the jails of Conakry, the return to Montmartre, dark years, alcohol and depression, a bistro bought with the proceeds from his contracts, old age, art as a way to forget. That was all Askia knew. The rest didn't matter. Petite-Guinée, agile despite his age, perched himself on a nearby stool. Askia gave him an account of the fire at the loft and the past few nights.

27

THE PARKING LOT. Deserted, dark, cold. He climbed into his cab and pulled his coat tight around his body. Sleep. At least an attempt at sleep. His foot nudging the accelerator. He told himself it would be a blessing to hit the gas and leave. His thoughts turned to Olia. She must be wondering where he was. He tried to conjure her up. Alone, the girl from Sofia, on this very sad, very beautiful night.

He imagined her. Sitting on the sofa, her gaze hovering vacantly over her books of photographs, the posters of her idols on the walls, the cups of coffee she had probably drunk, hoping something new would come up on this dull night spent searching yet again for Sidi's portraits, to the point of exhaustion.

Then he visualized her, the photographer, lying on the sofa with a book over her face to shield her eyes from the light, her feet resting on the box of a pizza that she had had trouble finishing. She had left the lights on because in the dark the zombies would come out to frighten her with their half-burned faces. She could not sleep. Because as soon as she shut her eyes, what she saw was terrifying. Masked heads smashing her door down, ripping the photos of her idols off the living room walls, carrying them off to be burned in a city square. She stood up and tried to stop them. She blocked the way with her thin body, but the masked men took away the pictures of Richard Wright, Ella Fitzgerald, Malcolm X, and the others. They went up to the mezzanine and scoured it until they found Sidi's portraits. They shouted:

"We've got him!"

"It took a while but we've got him!"

"He thought he could hide in the stillness of a few black-and-white pictures!"

He pictured Olia, eyes open, scanning the ceiling the way he would sometimes do. From time to time she heard footsteps on the stairway and hoped it was someone who had come to visit her. But the steps stopped one floor below and she concluded that it was her downstairs neighbour. That maybe none of this was real. That the steps she heard were in her troubled mind, that the turbaned man returning to Paris, asking for lodging, food, and water to wash his feet, was all an invention of hers.

The footsteps stopped. It was not Sidi. No one knocked. In a rage she sent the pizza box flying against the door and went up to the mezzanine. Finally she could not bear it any longer. Disregarding the late hour, she put on her boots, grabbed her coat, and ran out. She hailed a cab and took it to the wreck of the burnt building. She roamed the neighbourhood for a good two hours, walked around the building several times, came back to the front and concentrated on the shutters of the top floor, where the loft was. Hoping for something. An apparition. That the man with the turban would stick out his head and tell her he agreed to another photo session, another attempt to fix his movements in the face of any and all fires. But the stranger was not at the window. So it occurred to her to go to the plazas, the city squares, where a few illegals could always be found loitering. The stranger might be there — alive, burned, or dead.

She flagged down another cab. She found, in the middle of the Beaubourg square, a man. Alone. A countryman, dressed like Sidi. His hands were stuffed in the pockets of his coat, which he wore over his boubou, his head was bent, and his eyes studied the pavement like a beaten man. She ran towards him.

He turned and looked at her. She was disappointed
— this was not the man she sought. Nevertheless, she
questioned him:

"Have you seen a turban?"

". . ."

"I mean Sidi."

". . ."

From his coat the man pulled out a long shep-
herd's knife. No, not a knife, but a crippled hand that
he raised above his head.

"The turban, he's dead!"

"You mean Sidi?" she asked.

"Yes, Sidi."

"How do you know he's dead?"

"Simple deduction. You can't find him. So he's
dead."

28

BLACK NIGHT. The dark sheet of the sky. Askia left the parking lot and went for a drive. Over to the dead end where he would routinely stop for a break. Down a long avenue, three or four turns, a big man in a curbside phone booth yelling at the top of his lungs, a cobblestone lane smelling of urine and blind alleys. Blind alleys and muffled noises. It was hard to see ahead of him. A blurred view of black jackets and shaved heads. Busy making a muffled noise. Busy hitting. Kicking someone in the ribs. The sound grew more distinct. A length of steel chain flashing in the cab's headlights. Groans. He revved up his engine. The three men turned around, charged towards the cab, cursing loudly as they ran past. The steel chain striking the trunk.

He stopped. In the dead end, the man by the wall tried to stand up. Then he collapsed again on his right side. His head bloody. Opening one eye, he felt obliged to explain:

"Romania."

"I'll take you to the hospital."

"Romania."

"You're bleeding. I'll . . ."

"No. No hospital."

"It's not far."

"No."

The Rom left him there in the dead end and hobbled away. He was afraid of the hospital, of the questions they might ask there. Or at the police station: "How did you enter the country?"

The Rom, his bloody head. A red ball. As on that maliciously sunny day when he had managed to beat the dog Pontos on the head with a chunk of hard mortar. For weeks it dragged its wound around the garbage dump in Trois-Collines. Askia wanted to give it time to heal before striking again. And Father Lem was never there to protect his dog with the peculiar name, the name of some obscure divinity. An unsettling omen. A sign that the children would soon abandon Trois-Collines for the high seas and adventure. No, it wasn't the dog — it was the dog's name he disliked.

He tried to get some rest. His seat would not tilt back properly. A snag in the release mechanism underneath. He forced it. Nothing. Broken. He decided to change positions, leaving his bum in the driver's seat while dropping his upper body down on the passenger side. He ended up with his face against the glove compartment, his knees against the dashboard, and his feet underneath. An awkward position. Something nagged at his lower back. He tried to think. No use. An idea, just one, hovered in front of his eyes before rooting itself inside him: everything — the city, the blind alley, his cab — was going to blow up. It would start in the belly of the Earth; the pavement would lift up; every component of the street would be reduced to rubble and then propelled into the grey sky. It would be expertly done, with no trace left but the words on the last page: *End of Story*.

29

BUT THE PHOTOGRAPHER would not be put off and often repeated, "Who are you, Askia?" As if the answer to that question would somehow affect their relationship, as if a few clarifications would make him more familiar, less distant in the eyes of his friend. As if, in order to take part in the Wedding of the worlds, it was necessary to know who you were. It was necessary to be something or someone. Otherwise the king of the Wedding would reach out his hideous hand into the hall of festivities and banish you from the fete. Like the paws of that big bouncer who had shoved him away from the entrance of the discotheque where he had ventured one night when he was feeling blue. "You won't get in if you don't follow the dress code!" the bouncer had bellowed.

"Who are you, Askia?" The question took him back such a long way it was impossible to say for sure whether any of it was real. Back to the country roads and city streets, the foursome advancing through the fog, in the sweltering days and cold nights: he, his father, his mother, and the donkey, which eventually gave up the ghost. From Nioro du Sahel they had gone down to the Atlantic coast, leaving behind the most badly parched lands, but the beast had used up its last ounce of strength. It died as they came out of a muddy ravine. Had it been able to cover a few more roads, it would have found water and grass in the north of the country where they landed one grey dawn.

For a solid week they rested by the roadside. His mother, Kadia Saran, sold her medicinal roots and they were able to buy food. The terrible harmattan of 1967 was blowing itself out, its cutting edge growing duller on the skin. So they pushed on towards the plateaus, the centre of the new country that was to become theirs, and arrived in a village where the hospitality with which they were received surprised them. Askia thought the reason they had been shunned along the way was because those they encountered hadn't much to offer strangers,

or because the strangers to whom they had offered
shelter and yams turned into outright thieves after
nightfall. But he would never comprehend the reason
for their exodus. Perhaps the cause was not the sparse
rainfall or the swarms of locusts, as he had supposed.
Instead it may have been what his mother mentioned
one day. A matter of humiliation, according to the
mysterious words she alone knew how to wield. She
said, without elaborating, that his father, a Songhai
prince, had been humiliated by his own people. Or
possibly it was that he had wanted to avoid humiliation. Why? His mother, closing the chapter, said,
"Such things are best forgotten, Askia."

In the village of the plateaus they were given shelter by Chief Gokoli. An abandoned hut at the entrance
of the community, near the perimeter of an old cemetery with crumbling tombstones. An unhoped-for
refuge after the Sahel and the roads of flight. They
did not go out for three days, but the chief had fruit
and boiled yams brought to them. Three days in the
adobe hut. And when on the fourth day they walked
down the main road of the village, they were called
"Dirty Feet." It was said they had trekked over many
roads from the Sahel. The feet of the man in the turban and his family were caked with dirt and bleached
by the mud and dust of all the roads they had tramped
over. They had been subjected to heatwaves, rains,

the monsoon, and the harmattan. It was the harmattan that was to blame for their cracked heels, their parched, creased skin. And in the creases there was dirt, a mixture of sweat and earth. The voices on the main street whispered:

"Can it be that their feet are dirty because they could not stop walking?"

"Well, they were able to stop, as you can see."

"They've stopped in our village!"

"Because they can't or won't go any farther."

"Farther is the coast, the sea."

"And amidst the waves there's a malevolent god who ensnares gullible souls with an enticing call to voyage. His name is Pontos."

"A call."

"Enticing."

"Over there, across the ocean, it will be like the Kingdom of Heaven. You will live in a palace that looks out onto everlasting pleasures. To speak in more practical terms, you will no longer be hungry."

"A call."

"Alluring."

"And when the gullible creatures embark on the waves, the divinity of the seas devours them."

"These people are not gullible."

30

AT THE BISTRO he did not drink. He waited for Petite-Guinée, who had promised to take him to Sidi's building. He leaned against the counter, not wanting to sit down and yield to the temptation of a drink. Or cajole the barman so that he would play Miles Davis again for him. Or try to follow the notes as they rose towards the ceiling through the whorls floating up from the smoky corner of a pair of lips. Or ask for another drink to drive the first one deeper into the maze of his doubts. He did not want to drink at all, because on this night he had to remain absolutely clear-headed.

Petite-Guinée came out of his cellar through the hatch located behind the bar. He was wearing a leather jacket and a grey cap. They took the metro. Fifteen minutes later they emerged from the belly of Lutetia in front of Sidi's building. Petite-Guinée glanced around quickly, waited a few moments, then headed straight towards the entrance of the building. Askia stayed by the metro staircase. Petite-Guinée pulled a tool from his pocket and began to work the lock of the makeshift door that must have been installed after the fire. The lock quickly gave way, which erased any remaining doubts Askia may have harboured as to the old man's background and skills. Petite-Guinée waved him over and closed the door behind them, and with the help of a flashlight that he had slipped into his jacket pocket, they went straight up to the loft.

The scene was grim. The steps were slippery with a fine layer of ash, the walls were sooty, and a strange odour permeated the air. One had the distinct impression of being in the mouth of a mine shaft. They went up. Askia was surprised by the stamina of his friend, who never paused to catch his breath. The loft finally came into view. Astonishingly unencumbered. The pillars were oddly clean. The beam of the flashlight swept over the walls, starting from the nearest corner to their left and then covering the entire space, as if seeking to shed light on the mystery of every surface in the dark loft. Secrets. Things and beings buried in the shadows: a precious casket, a man hidden behind the concrete partitions.

They followed the lighted arc curving and moving back and forth in the space and the silence of the walls. In front of them the Songhai frescos, three-quarters destroyed. Petite-Guinée sighed and carried on with his inspection. The meddling flashlight illuminated the shadows, the secrets of that corner on the right, where a rustling noise made them both jump. The shadow leaped forward, brushing against Petite-Guinée's jacket before scurrying away. Askia dashed after it into the black hole of the stairway where it had disappeared. When he finally got outside, the shadow was turning the corner of the first street on the right. He glimpsed something falling from the flounces of her long white dress, little pieces of cardboard that turned out to be train tickets bought in various cities, some far away — Matera, Coimbra, Naples, Saragossa — others nearer — Marseilles, Nantes . . .

Petite-Guinée came out behind him and shut the door. He said there was nothing up there but mysteries and shadows. Among the tickets that had fallen from the shadow's pocket, the one from Nantes seemed ancient, printed in another century, at the beginning of the mass insanity that had cast people out on the road. Beings belonging to Askia's kind, when other niggers named Sidi were bartered for a double-barrelled shotgun and expelled from Ouidah, Saint-Louis du Sénégal, to be shipped as slaves and deported ultimately to Virginia.

31

A FIELD IN Virginia, the journey's endpoint, where the curse could finally be played out. Collapse in the weariness and emptiness of the body of Sidi's great-great-great-great-grandfather, who bore the same forename, which on arriving in Virginia he was forced to relinquish in exchange for the ludicrous moniker of Waldo. Meanwhile, another Sidi put out to sea in Guinea as the manservant of a shipowner and ended up loading crates in Nantes before the slave ship weighed anchor for the trading posts of Gorée, Joal-la-Portugaise, Assinie, Coromantin, Winneba, Fort Saint-Antoine, Mitumbo, Saint-Georges de la Mine, and Gwato, where the voyage began again.

In the entrails of the slave ship, Sidi the slave

ancestor hoisted a heavy bale on his back, climbed
up on the deck, and found himself facing a lady who
was standing on the wharf in the shade of a tiny parasol. Salt breeze. Grey waves. The two individuals
eyed each other. Surreptitiously. Around them, a bee-
hive of activity. Traders and shipowners, the noise
of unloading and, farther along, beyond the docks,
shuttered buildings and silent streets. The lady with
the parasol saw this man, Askia's great-great-great-
great-great-grandfather, and felt certain urges. She
saw herself being fucked by the fury of the ancestor,
who meanwhile wondered how it would be to ven-
ture into the belly of the parasol, if it would be like
exploring the open forest of his Keidou, the generous one, with whom he had fathered a clutch of kids
before being captured in the Gulf of Guinea early one
cynical morning.

He set his bale down on the deck and began to
arrange crates as the parasol looked on. Steadily.
She followed his movements, his heavy chest bending over, crashing into a body she imagined was her
own, stretched out on the deck.

Eventually she walked away, and the ancestor,
watching her out of the corner of his eye, saw her disappear into the corridors formed by the large crates
and barrels arrayed in blocks in preparation for loading. He left the deck and followed her. Caught sight

of the edge of the lady's white dress just as she turned a corner. Hurried over and found her on the floor of desire, a big crate full of boards, her genitals offered up like a crêpe.

"My name is Camille," she told him before squeezing him between her thighs. Soon, crying out, he poured the water and butter of his pain into Camille's crêpe. And inside Camille's crêpe he sowed the blighted seed that, centuries later, would continue to people the suburbs with dirty-footed bastards forever railing against the skies.

It happened on the docks of Nantes, and afterwards the parasol and the ancestor returned to their respective spheres.

32

IT WAS LATE when Askia and Petite-Guinée returned from their fruitless excursion into the ruins of the loft. Midnight had come and gone, and a breeze nibbled at their faces, prompting them to hurry over to Montmartre, where Petite-Guinée wanted to show something to his friend — his intimate country tucked away in the depths, where he believed he had resolved the question of his constant urge to run away. Somehow Askia found the tranquil, silent winter night beautiful. They went back to the bar with the understated facade where the wooden door stood out against the grey beige of the roughcast. The old man said they would go down to the cellar. Askia was under the impression that, as usual, Petite-Guinée wanted him, his only public, to see a drawing in his workshop.

They slipped behind the bar and went through the hatch that led to a stone staircase whose steps had become polished over the years. Askia shivered when he touched the slightly damp walls. He could not get used to it, even though this was not the first time he had come this way. They reached the first landing, where to the right there was another opening: the cellar door, behind which Petite-Guinée painted his pictures. But the master of the house passed this door by. They continued to descend and arrived at the very bottom, in front of a third door. Petite-Guinée inserted a massive iron key. It opened the moment the timer on the stairs shut off the lights, plunging them into pitch-darkness. The old man swore at the timing device, which must have been malfunctioning. But he nevertheless managed to feel his way to the corner of the wall directly inside the entrance, and a dusty fluorescent light filled the space.

It was a minuscule room, measuring no more than eight square metres. The ceiling was very low, the walls were porous, and the floor was covered with red slabs. In the middle stood a large wooden table that at one time must have been a family dining table. On it were little cards, that is, photographs. Petite-Guinée, who had not spoken for many minutes, said, "I want you to look, Askia."

". . ."

"And to appreciate this little room where I've installed my country."

". . ."

Askia focused on the table. On it were photos of girls and boys who were barely adolescents. Portraits of children. On the back of each picture was a given name: *Kadia, Feyla, Chinga, Cabral.* Askia didn't get it. The events in the photos meant nothing to him. Petite-Guinée, who was close behind him, spoke up. Those children's faces, he said, their smiles — he had stolen them. In 1969. That year he was in Biafra. On which side? On both. He had worked for the rebels and the government. In arms. It was exciting to have signed contracts with both sides. Because he saw that none of it made any sense, that in time the anger would cool down, and during that time the arms dealers and mercenaries would stuff their pockets. He hadn't invented the Biafra War, nor the ones before and after. He needed to tell himself this to be able to go on, to convince himself that he wasn't more of a shit than anyone else. To pass the time between deliveries he would take a few pictures of the landscape and the children. Because they were beautiful, the little ones. His lens stole the innocence of their faces ravaged by war. He figured that later the pictures would help him decide to stop. Did he become attached to the faces, the land, the countries that weren't supposed to mean anything but contracts, deliveries, such-and-such, a place on his job list? He said that Africa was a passage. For him, for those who'd come before him, for those still going down there and those yet to come. New warlocks come from near or far would pass by there again to re-colonize the niggers.

In the country of his cellar he tried to put an end to the torment of his soul. Askia looked once again at the pictures of the children. Petite-Guinée had gone quiet. Tired out. They climbed back up the stone stairway.

"Askia, it's boiling inside me and I can't control it."

"The emotions?"

"Whenever I go down to look at those photographs. It hits me in the gut and galls my skin every time."

At the bar he served them both a whisky. Outside, through the gap between the curtains, Askia caught a glance of the white shadow spying on them, perhaps trying to retrieve her train tickets.

33

HE WENT BACK to work wishing for a final meeting with the shadow. One more night, the last act of the dying winter. Once out of the parking lot, he turned right at the first corner. He had driven barely a hundred metres when a man flagged him down. It was unusual, especially at night, to pick up a fare so quickly. He found this piece of luck somewhat odd but could not turn it down. He hoped the client would be the friendly sort, someone he could have a conversation with. The man wore a hat. He settled into the back of the car, removed his headgear. Silence.

"How's it going, Askia?"

". . ."

Askia recognized him. The man in the back seat chuckled.

"It's good to see you again."

". . ."

"I must say, you haven't changed."

"You neither."

"Thanks. For the compliment."

"It's not a compliment. Just the truth. You haven't changed, Zak."

"Yeah, but it's been a while, Askia. Lots of water and a few corpses under the bridge. And through our hands."

". . ."

"And here you are, in this city so foreign to what we were. I guess you left, deserted, because you thought this city, the night here, which knows nothing of your past, could protect you. But you know very well that the past is like a woman who's in love with you and won't leave you alone. Your new situation doesn't change a thing. Sorry, friend. Believe me, I would have preferred to meet you under different circumstances and celebrate another kind of Mass."

". . ."

"Like meet you for a drink, have some fun the way we used to, or just shoot the breeze, sitting on the hoods of our cabs after the night shift. But life is cruel. Isn't it, Askia?"

" . . . "

"You can't always choose the Mass you're going to celebrate. You want to stay a choirboy, pure and innocent in your white robe, but then you end up playing the monster. I understand. It was hard work, and eventually it got to you. You're human. I understand and I respect that. But you know that in our case it's better to blow yourself away than to run away. Don't you think it's better?"

" . . . "

"You're out of luck, Askia. We found you. This really isn't the best town to hole up in. Did you forget that it's called the City of Lights? You can't hide in the light . . . Sorry."

" . . . "

"I'm telling you this because we respected each other. Otherwise I would have finished the job by now, but I find this contract repugnant — knocking off a colleague. I see it as another role, a new one, one more after all the roles we've had to play. It's a character role, something completely original; for once, you'll be the choirboy. Let's go. Drive, my friend. Go to that wood — you know, where the night shoots its wad in the bellies of the *filles de joie*."

Askia did not have to wonder whether the man was pointing his weapon at him. It was a basic precaution. And Zak — the Terrible, they used to call him — had always been very efficient. He had joined the Cell before Askia and had shown him the ropes. The reflexes and moves needed to be good at what you did. Meticulous. Zak seemed to be thinking. For a moment Askia heard nothing. He spoke up:

"What have you been up to, Zak?"

"What have I been up to?"

"Yeah."

"Let's say I haven't been able to make a career change like you. I'm still . . . you know."

"And the others? What about them?"

Zak coughed.

"The others . . . Some stayed, some got out; a lot of them are dead."

"You mean eliminated."

"Dead. Camilio was found in a ditch with his stomach ripped open; Martin, burned to a crisp behind the wheel of his car . . ."

"Maybe accidents?"

"Lika hanged himself. Leo got married to a colonel's daughter. Now he's got a nice house and a big family. Upward mobility, you might say. Tino, the old guy, the veteran, he's retired and spends his days on a seafront terrace drinking pastis. Carno lost his mind and walks around naked in the alleys of the old market. Faustin is getting contracts in North America; John's on the run. That pretty much covers the old crew. How far are we from the wood? You know, Askia, the sooner this gets done the better. Sorry, friend."

34

HE PARKED AT the edge of the wood. Zak ordered
him to get out of the car and walk ahead of him.
This is what Askia did, and they advanced through
the trees. A milky moon in a clear night sky. Zak
told him to turn around and step towards him. He
obeyed. Zak, his arm fully extended, held his pistol
level with Askia's head. Askia walked towards him.
He could not see his face: the other man had lowered
his hat over his eyes. A trace of wind came up. Askia
concentrated on the wind, on its trace. He received
a blow in the stomach. He did not register anything
akin to pain. He found himself down on his knees.
Then Zak's voice sounded: "You've gone soft, Askia.
All I did was push you. Lie down."

Now he was lying on his back, immobile, with the cool grass underneath him. Already dead. Zak swore: "Damn it, I still have to do this bit! I don't like taking pictures of the stiff, but — and you know this — I have to bring back proof that I finished the job. Oh well, you're almost dead anyway. They won't notice the difference. I'll take the pictures and then . . . There's no way I'm going to put a stiff in my camera."

Askia was struck in the face by a kind of light, a flash. Zak repeated this a dozen times. Capturing the moment. Askia heard one more click, the flash. Zak sighed. "Goodbye, my friend."

Askia closed his eyes. Waited. The shot hit him right in the face. The shot. Zak's booming laughter, his voice:

"Gotcha! Admit it, Askia, I really had you."

". . ."

Zak was in stitches.

"Tell me, do you really believe I'd go through that whole song and dance to finish you off? Hey, you should have seen yourself. Come on, tell me, what does it feel like? Eh? What's it like living your last moments?"

". . ."

"You don't want to get up?"

Askia could barely grasp what was happening. He lay glued to the grass, trying to persuade himself that this could not be a joke — Zak was toying with him, playing with his nerves. Then Zak told him that he too had deserted. He had had enough — the routine of murder had worn him out. But what had finally pushed him over the edge was what he had said in the taxi: the guys started to disappear. Mysteriously. He didn't understand. There were rumours about goings-on inside the Cell. It felt strange to go over to the other side, to become the prey, he said. Like a wedge of cold iron in your gut. He had been obliged to slip into a woman's body. A disguise to get across the border in the north. After that, a long journey: Bobo-Dioulasso, Bamako, Niamey, Tripoli, Tunis, Malta, Athens . . . How had he managed? He would tell him another time. Askia was stretched out on the grass. His face was suddenly struck by a light, but from a different source. He opened his eyes. The headlights of a car that must have been parked at the edge of the wood. Then a voice, very loud: "Identify yourself!"

Zak whistled. "Shit! See you later, friend. Be careful, the Cell is looking for us!" At this point he punched Askia in the face. The light grew stronger. Zak fled, vanishing into the shadows behind Askia. Into the night. Askia heard footsteps on the grass. He sat up and shifted backwards on his rear end. He raised his elbow, trying to shield his eyes against the beam of the flashlight. The policeman questioned him. He had been cruising when he saw quick flashes of light in the wood. His partner ran up behind him. Askia explained that a thief had mugged him and tried to kill him. He had picked him up thinking he was an ordinary fare. The policeman with the flashlight held out his hand. He clasped it and hoisted himself to his feet. The officer told him he'd been lucky. Probably his number hadn't come up. Once he had lodged a complaint, Askia could go to the hospital to have them take care of the bump over his right eye. He would have to follow them to the station in his cab. The one who had found him shone the light on his face again. He wanted to make sure he was not too badly beaten. But Askia wasn't listening. He was far away. Isolated in a cell. Inside the walls of the past.

35

THE CELL WAS a murky organization. Unofficial intelligence body, militia specialized in kidnapping, torture, and murder. The standard mission statement. Askia was a member and his role was to keep things under control. To keep the populace quiet. He had volunteered for this work, which involved total engagement in what was, what is a program of purges. He was to observe and report, and in the course of many nights on the job he had become a ripper, whose weapons were his efficiency, his hands, a revolver, a belt of explosives, a taxi called "The Passage," a steadfast will, ironclad insensitivity, and indifference.

He had joined on an October night in 1984 because the money was good. Just what was needed to avoid relying on his student bursary, which came as often as rain in the desert. Just what was needed to fatten up that all too paltry purse. Just what was needed to pay for the operation on a sick mother, exhausted by housework in other people's homes in the real city perched high above their slum. But in the lower part of town the mother breathed her last, and the son's ultimate efforts to raise the money for an operation were left hanging.

The Cell. He was to be a cab driver like any other. Pick up fares and ask them harmless questions. And if they turned out to be rebels who found fault with the government, eliminate them, silence the stinking mouths whose words were fouling the atmosphere. Tarnishing the country's name and image. People incapable of truly loving the country because they had no country. Troublemakers. Vermin. Schemers, enemies, envious of the nation's accomplishments — that is what the Powers said of them. And how could they not be envious, since they had no nation. He was to eliminate all the political adventurers. With the night and the darkness as accomplices. He had his badge and he moved like a cat among the shadows. Or rather, he had to make the night his element and make a career of hunting down idle, irresponsible globetrotters. His job: drive the rebels far outside the city, where the downtown lights were no longer visible, where his passengers could not be seen, strap the explosive belt onto them, and, sitting in his taxi-cab, push the button.

His past. A deserted night, an empty lot, a vehicle in the night, the driver holding a box, a red button, a finger — more specifically, the thumb — on the button, the thumb pressing down on the button and the adventurer's belly exploding just a stone's throw from the taxi. A death dirge to decorate the silence of the streets and the ghosts' laments.

Because that was what he was — a maker of ghosts and death works. The suspect passengers, the ones he made disappear, had to be dispossessed of the thick-ness of the living. They became a mirage of the liv-ing. Nonentities. Removed from the thickness of life. Of the nation. They became, like his father, vague traces, sketches in pencil or black ink stains, stillborn portraits, unformed sculptures into which the artist had not had time to breathe life. He was an artist of death who, during his childhood in Trois-Collines, had been able to practise on the dog Pontos.

36

ASKIA THOUGHT BACK to his flight, to what he had
done to extricate himself from the murderous night.
After years of hunting down the enemies of the
nation, he had moved into a different field. A new
specialty. He became a bodyguard. The Cell offered
various positions according to one's tastes and apti-
tudes: tailing, interrogation, assassination, close
protection. The Cell was bursting with talent. Askia
was assigned to protect important people. People
who mattered. Who made decisions. Who travelled
because they needed to expand their network. He
waited. Impatient as a fledgling waiting for the bap-
tismal sky, for flight. Three months into the new job,
the politician he was guarding was given a mission.

Askia never learned what it was. It was that kind of mission. They landed at Charles de Gaulle in Paris. For him this was a new beginning. He would hold on, tooth and nail, to the pavement of exile. Two days after they arrived, taking advantage of his night off, he left the hotel on Rue de Rivoli where the members of the mission were staying. He put the Cell behind him, crossed the line. That's what they said in the Cell whenever one of them deserted. His college friend Tony, who lived in the Barbès district, was expecting him. He had been able to leave the country thanks to a scholarship. For six months Askia holed up there, going out only rarely, at night. Tony had warned him: Paris wasn't the best place to hide from the Cell. He thought Askia should go farther away, across the Atlantic, to America — some forsaken Caribbean island or a backcountry town in Maryland. Or to Montreal, where Tony knew people who could help his friend, people who never responded when he wrote to them.

Askia touched the spot above his eye — the swelling had gone down somewhat. Zak had not punched him very hard. Just enough for the cops to believe his story. Apparently it was nothing serious. The cops had taken his deposition, his charges against X, and he had left the station.

He took an ointment out of his first-aid kit and

rubbed it on the bruise. Back behind the wheel, he thought about the charges. Against X. And he smiled. Because he had been an X. A no-name driver. Like Zak, in those Cell cabs, planting death in the heart of the tropical night.

He decided not to go back to work. There was someone he wanted to see. Monsieur Ali of Port Said, a no-name with whom he occasionally chatted. He had met Monsieur Ali by the Auguste-Comte entrance of the Jardin du Luxembourg, directly across the way from Olia's apartment. Monsieur Ali, the chestnut vendor. He had smiled at Askia and gone back to roasting his chestnuts, making sure not to burn them. It was late, the tourists were gone, but Monsieur Ali could not stop roasting chestnuts. He made paper cones, which he then filled with chestnuts. He used newsprint or pages torn out of old books. He put ten roasted chestnuts in each cone and charged two euros a cone. Monsieur Ali of Port Said was there, preparing cones of chestnuts for the tourists, and Askia sat down near him on the curb. The chestnuts were cooking on the grill. From time to time Monsieur Ali of Port Said fanned the embers. He said he made paper cones and pyramids so as not to forget the country of his father. It made him happy when he succeeded in shaping a beautiful large cone.

Monsieur Ali had survived, thousands of miles from his home, thanks to those cones and pyramids that he fashioned to stay in touch with history. In 1968, when he had arrived in France, the wind of Port Said was still on his face. He wanted to be a teacher. To teach the poetry of Abu Nuwas and the suras in the West. But minds were being seduced by a different music and new words, rock and the poems of Allen Ginsberg. Seducing a generation with long, dirty hair, outraged at the establishment, like those unwashed hippies in a California park wallowing in a disgusting orgy. Preferring dirty love to the violence of military boots in the Vietnam War.

Monsieur Ali had seen rock music engulf the words of Abu Nuwas. So he became a street vendor. He moved around to avoid sitting in some station where he might catch cold. To keep moving, he sold chestnuts from Gonesse to Boulogne. And Port Said slipped farther and farther away. Port Said and Abu Nuwas. So he made paper pyramids on Boulevard Saint-Michel in order not to forget. Monsieur Ali was a man of few words.

37

OLIA TOOK THE remote control, turned on the TV, surfed the channels, turned it off, then on again, surfed, turned it off. She was anxious. She had never lost a piece of her work. Sidi's portraits must surely be somewhere. Still, she began to have doubts, and Askia reminded her that Sidi was a shadow. She sighed, exhausted, laid her head on her friend's shoulder, shut her eyes.

"You ought to go up and get some rest," he advised.

"My legs are numb. Does it bother you to lend me your shoulder?"

"Shoulders aren't very comfortable."

She seemed not to hear him anymore. Maybe she was not pretending but was truly weary, drained.

Again he spoke to her but received no response. He gave her a little shake. No response, just a murmur and some purring. Finally he decided to carry her upstairs. He lifted her up. She wrapped her arms around his neck and placed her head on his chest. On the fourth step leading to the mezzanine he almost stumbled. He caught himself, instinctively planting his right foot on the next step in front of him, just barely preventing a fall. Otherwise he would have had to pick up the pieces of her brittle body from the floor.

She tightened her grip around his neck. They managed to reach the room. He was obliged to clear a path through the framed pictures strewn over the floor. Then he climbed up the wooden stairway leading to the platform on which the bed stood, a metre below the ceiling. He put her on the bed. Next to the pillow was a balled-up blanket, which he spread over her. She looked very small under the blanket. Her lips murmured something, and Askia heard the words within himself: "I looked in my boxes. He wasn't there. There's nothing in my boxes, no trace of an event or a face that was . . . There's nothing in the boxes, Askia. I searched and I started to put new things in them, a few items. Because we can always leave again if the urge comes back."

She had spoken with her eyes closed the whole time. Now she was asleep. Askia walked out of the room and went to the bathroom to relieve himself. He looked at the ceiling. Through one of the panes in the skylight he could see a bit of clear, transparent sky, and he wanted to inhale it. He pushed open the skylight. The air chilled his face. He rose up on his tiptoes and contemplated a few roofs pierced by chimneys blowing white smoke into the scene. They were solitary mouths open to the sky, not just to breathe but to swallow, to glean . . . he did not know what exactly. Like the orphaned mouths of the kids in the lanes of his childhood.

He went back down to the living room. To do the same thing as Olia. Sleep a little.

But sleep did not come. He felt hot. He went back up to the bathroom to take a proper shower. Then perhaps he would feel better. He stripped off his clothes and dropped them on top of the laundry hamper. The water did him good. He worked up a thick lather, using the foam to massage the painful areas on his ribs. Then he went back to the living room and turned on the television. The journalist on TF1 spoke quickly. He reported that a man had been found dead in a downtown parking lot. His throat had been slit. A photo of the victim flashed across the screen and Askia recognized Zak, who had come to Paris to be forgotten by the Cell. The journalist described the crime as gruesome because the body had been dismembered. The legs, most conspicuously, had been sawed off, in keeping with some strange ritual. To keep the dead man from running in the afterlife? The Cell did not fool around. The journalist spoke quickly. More news and personalities streamed by on the TV screen.

38

ASKIA DID NOT want to remain a character, like the puppet that danced at the command of a busker on the sidewalks of the real city, the downtown area where he would stroll as a teenager. The puppet was called Abuneke, a little man made of scraps of cloth. He would go to see the routine and follow the story of the cloth man. This was something he did when the films at Le Togo Theatre did not seem very appealing. The show was held outdoors in front of the old savings bank, by the side of a road that teemed with life day and night. The puppeteer worked his marionette with nylon strings that were hardly noticeable in the shifting twilight. The man told an ancient story of exodus, the one about the Ewe people's march from Egypt through Oyo in Nigeria to the Gulf of Guinea. The story was conveyed through the mouth and movements of Abuneke: bowing to the crowd, wagging his head, spinning his head all the way around to grab the public's attention, arms flung out in counterpoint to the legs that danced, hopped, wandered around while the arms traced a strange figure in the air — an infinite road — with an invisible baton.

Not to remain a character, an Abuneke bound to genealogy by strings. To become something else, a cold image or — why not? — a statue, frozen in the world of stone. So when he walked through the streets of Paris he made the biblical gesture, turning around in the hope of being turned to stone.

39

RESTLESS NIGHT. Dreaming again that he had found Sidi. In Cité Rose. A posh neighbourhood for the nouveau riche, once a shantytown where he had lived with his mother. The slum area had been razed a few years before and its inhabitants forced to leave and find shelter elsewhere, to push farther into the new outlying zones.

He was in the cemetery that lay on the perimeter of Cité Rose. The cemetery: the only place that had survived from the past. Sidi's grave was there, in a corner by the fence that was to the right as you entered. He sat down on the tombstone, at the end where his father's head must be. Facing Sidi, whom he had finally found. He felt no particular emotion.

He looked at the dead man lying with his eyes closed in his sepulchre. What were his eyelids shutting out? Was he ashamed? Of what?

The tomb was isolated. There was bare red earth around it. The other sepulchres stood several metres away. Silently. Eventually Sidi opened his eyes and looked at him. He was calm, serene. Guessing the question in his son's gaze, he offered what could be taken as an answer: "I wanted to find my cousin Camara Laye at Aubervilliers. At the Simca factory. When I arrived on that dreary afternoon in the fall of 1971, they told me he was no longer there. Gone. After that I kept moving. It's a passion of mine — the road. Our road. The only one we have." And he began to laugh. The sepulchre shook. So did the surrounding neighbourhood and the whole city. The other dead grumbled in their resting places: "Sidi, when will you, along with your nomad offspring, leave us in peace? You wouldn't by any chance envy us for being at rest, would you? You can't sleep — we know that. You're always turning." The sepulchre quaked again. The tombstone moved. Sidi showed him a road map. And ordered him: "Get going, Telemachus! Hit the road! For whatever reason suits you!"

40

HE THOUGHT OF Zak again, hunted down by the Cell. Zak had been quick to grasp that it was game over, that Paris would not protect him anymore, that he would have to travel farther north, although that would just be a way of delaying the execution. He had harked back to all the people they had murdered in their cabs. And so he had drawn the conclusion that this turn of events was fair, to the point that it was senseless to decamp any farther towards the polar latitudes.

Consequently, Zak had come back to the square of the church where he was in the habit of going around in circles, searching for the way to deliverance. He had sat down on the paving stones right in the middle of the square, stretched out his legs, and placed the flat of his hands on the pavement, like a lover who is reluctant to leave. He knew this was the best way to close the book of his undoing: to behave like a man who wants to stay connected to the stones and smells of a place. To sit there a good part of the day, pretending to abide in the place of his migration. Time passed, nighttime arrived together with a cold wind, a street lamp came on, two men stepped into the square. They dragged him to the parking lot and chopped him up.

That was how Askia pictured Zak's last moments, the final chapter of the book of his friend's flight.

He left the apartment on Rue Auguste-Comte and returned to the parking lot, feeling he had found his solution. He did not get in behind the steering wheel. Instead he sat down with his back leaning against a pillar and waited. Hoping to end like Zak. He unfolded his limbs, stretching his legs out on the cement, stretching his arms out along his thighs. To offer up his body to whatever violence happened to come along. He was not aware of the cold. He would not count on that to kill him. It would be more brutal.

He checked his watch. At least an hour had gone by with him sitting in this position. Nothing had happened. Then an idea occurred to him, one that could speed things up. He got up and ran over to his cab.

Rummaged through the glove compartment, where he had carelessly stuffed the money from his last fares. He took the cash and went back to the spot he had chosen for his torture and death. He tossed the money onto his stomach and all around his body. In plain sight. All that was left for him was to hope that a random passerby would take the money and kill him. He would make a show of putting up a fight, of violently resisting his aggressor, who would then have no choice but to act decisively.

At dawn a man arrived. Wearing a long coat and a felt hat. The hat slightly skewed over his left ear. A cigarette hung in his fist. A plume of smoke rose from the cigarette. The man walked with a limp. He looked like a veteran. A veteran of all the crimes he must have committed in the night, a veteran of the life that must have eaten up his leg. He stepped resolutely towards Askia. Askia stayed calm. There was an air of mystery surrounding the man. A magnificent picture: the long coat topped with the felt hat, which bent down, the cigarette smoking in his fist, the whole scene set against the background of an unreal night striped with rows of cars in the parking lot. He advanced. Would soon be touching Askia's feet. A splendid tableau. The only thing missing was a colour, in fact, two colours: the gleam of a blade catching the pale light in the parking lot and the red of the victim's blood.

The man touched Askia's feet. Plunged his hand into a pocket on the right side, froze for an instant, coughed, knelt down, touched the banknotes that rested on his stomach. Askia was ready. As soon as the man made another move, he would jump on him. Again the man coughed. Touched his chest. Askia closed his eyes. He could not see the aggressor. He could smell him. The man spoke: "Can I help you, sir? Would you like me to call the police? Have you been assaulted?"

The man shook his shoulder. Askia opened his eyes. "Everything's fine," he answered. "I'm an actor. I have to play a role — mine. I'm in training."

The man uttered a few words that Askia did not catch. He stood up and walked to his cab. Meanwhile the man went back to his Cadillac, which was parked on the far side of the pillar. Askia checked his watch. Five o'clock. Daybreak. It would not happen this time. On another night, maybe in the next movie, he would be killed like Zak. He started to laugh.

41

IN THE LATE afternoon he once again found Monsieur Ali of Port Said and his chestnuts. Business had been very slow and he had amused himself all day by making cones and pyramids out of wrapping paper. Dozens of them under a street lamp on Boulevard Saint-Michel. Another night already. Askia had spent the day trying not to think of Zak, telling himself it was better this way, that in any event his colleague could not have hoped for a better end.

He admired the innocence of the old man, who was full of hope, believing as he did that as long as he could sell roasted chestnuts he might be able to save enough money for passage back to Port Said, in which case he would always have his pyramids, his land of paper.

Askia formed a mental image of hope: a crazy man who had found refuge in Paris, dressed in rags, sitting under a street lamp creating a paper homeland to maintain the illusion of having somewhere to live. Henceforward Monsieur Ali inhabited the words of Abu Nuwas, which he recited in the blind alleys of Barbès and on the steps of Montmartre, overlooking the city. At two euros for a cone of chestnuts, he said, if he sold thirty cones he would be able to pay for a Chinese dinner at the Ni Hao on Rue de la Hachette, a night out of the cold in a filthy Clignancourt motel, and a calling card to try, as he had every night for fifty years, to reach a woman at a number in Port Said.

Askia left Monsieur Ali, who in the evening had a few customers to attend to. The alleys of the Latin Quarter were empty and sad, a black cat stood watch at a window, the dark mass of a roof blocked the horizon, and three men in black jackets were whooping it up three blocks down, where the alley melded with the wharves along the Seine. The closer he came, the more he could feel the reverberations of their party.

The three men were pounding on something. A drum sitting on the pavement. With what, Askia could not yet say. The skinheads jumped up, drew a deep breath before landing, and struck. They were using their feet too, and as Askia came closer, the steel studs on their jackets glinted in the night. Then he saw that they were beating the drum with steel bars, but the ritual that had delighted them a few minutes before now seemed to bore them. They stopped giggling. Their jumping diminished, the pavement stirred, the thing they were hitting rose from the ground, and Askia saw the turbaned head above the black jackets. It was white, the head, and for a brief moment it seemed to follow the festive rhythm of the leather jackets. It jerked in the wind, which made the turban fly off, and the skinheads again began to thump with their steel bars.

Askia heard a shriek. The black cat bounded into the lane and ran off towards the wharves. Nothing stirred on the pavement anymore. The three men picked up the body and cast it into the river before going their separate ways. The black cat returned to roll itself in the white cloth left behind by the poor wretch, but then it darted away like a child caught red-handed.

42

THE BLACK CAT had left him the white cloth as a gift, and he gathered it up off the ground. The surface of the water had gone smooth again, as if to signify that nothing had occurred, that Askia was the sole inventor of the scene he had just witnessed. In his hand the spotless cloth smelled of sweat, of a presence. He could not help sensing a kind of force behind him. Askia wheeled around and saw him on the wharf on the other side of the street.

He was wearing a costume — a collection of variously coloured cloths sewn together to form a robe — while a mask of wood and leather cloaked his head. The wood covered the face, and the leather portion was a hood enveloping the crown and the

back of the neck. The robe had a golden sheen and
bore the image of a shell on the breast. A luminous
aura surrounded the apparition. The feet were invisible inside an ample pair of stockings that comprised
the lower part of the costume. He resembled an egun
— a ghost. He began to dance, emitting little yelps,
spinning around, spreading out the skirt of his costume, hopping, floating the flounces of his robe on
the night wind, and most of all rotating on the axis
of his body, which he never managed to stabilize,
turning as if he were a planet, with starlike sequins
sewn onto the cloth. He executed little dance steps
in every direction, stepped back, and returned to the
starting point.

Askia was petrified. He knew what they were, the
eguns. Or rather he did not know. The eguns would
come on feast days to dance in the sacred forest on
the edge of the coastal city where he had grown up,
or in the village squares in Porto-Novo and Oyò and
the hamlets around Lake Togo. You were not supposed to see what — man or god — was concealed
under the cloth or raffia costume. The egun on the
wharf was hiding inside this costume, the mask of
his exile. He wished to remain wrapped in the cloak
of night, to disappear into its folds. He was enraged
because someone was following its every move.
Under no circumstances would he wish to go back

to the Sahel or the shores of a river down there to ask
for an explanation from the god Oya Igbalé. To ask
why he had been condemned to wander. He stopped
dancing, and when Askia went to cross the street to
meet him, the egun bolted towards the nearest metro
station.

Askia arrived at the entrance to the station, which
was closed. No sign of the egun.

43

IN HIS HANDS a strange object, the turban — relic of a time or a being that had been. He would tell Olia that he had found him. He keyed in the entrance code to the girl's building and found himself face to face with the concierge, who stopped him. "She has gone away, Mademoiselle Olia. She left a letter for you."

A beautiful night. Laughing stars. His hand was shaking. Standing on the sidewalk in front of his friend's building, he tried to make sense of her sudden exit. He looked around in every direction, wondering which way the girl from Sofia had gone. There were only a few possibilities: either end of this street, the building behind him, or the gates of the park across the street. He rubbed his eyes and discerned a silhouette in front of him. It resembled the one that had approached him in the parking lot, the night he had decided to end it all at the foot of the pillar.

The silhouette wore the same long coat and a hat. Askia recognized him. He had often noticed this man leaning against the fence of the Jardin du Luxembourg. A few times Askia had heard him ranting to himself. Olia one day said that the man had been coming there for years, repeating the same story, always with exactly the same ending: "I arrived in 1985. From East Berlin. They promised me. They said, 'Get across the Wall, go to the West, and you're saved.' I crossed the Wall. Nothing on the other side. No one. Maybe I should go back in the other direction."

Olia thought the man was demented. Once, as she walked out of her apartment with her Leica hanging across her shoulder, the man had stepped up and handed her a piece of paper with these words written on it:

> *And she threw into the camera*
> *Twenty gardens*
> *And the birds of Galilee*
> *And continued searching beyond the sea*
> *For a new meaning to truth.*

The man told Olia these were the words of the poet of the narrow land, Mahmoud Darwish. One of the Dirty Feet. He had smiled with his tobacco-yellowed teeth and disappeared into the crowd in the garden.

Askia was expecting the man to trot out the same East Berlin story. He was not shaking so much now, and he went to sit down in a corner to read Olia's letter. But the man, the silhouette in the long coat, was watching him, his hands covering his mouth. There was smoke rising from his face. The cigarette was burning between his lips. The lighter, which he had not bothered to extinguish, was in his left hand, close to the pocket of his coat, which at any moment could catch fire. The flame danced over the fabric and it seemed that his left side was quivering, twitching as though gripped by an attack, the nerves shuddering under the skin of the arm that held the flame.

It was difficult to see the man's face in the half-light. A face that must have been sneering — he could hear the snickering. He thought the man was going to tell him his story. The man was a shadow in front of the fence. The shadow raised its right hand to its hat and tapped it in a sort of salute, a show of respect before the speech that followed: "Good day, friend. I know you've had a hard day. Here you are, heir to a piece of white cloth. In other words, a blank page, with no footprints for you to step into. Heir to emptiness! It's hard, this city, isn't it. Everything leaves here, everything escapes, people pass through. She's left, the girl, hasn't she. She must not be the kind that stays."

The man moved away from the fence and went off towards the metro on the Boulevard Saint-Michel.

Askia sat down on the curb. Had the man been referring to Olia? Had he possibly seen her leave? He stood up again. To run after the man and ask him if he had seen his friend. But he had second thoughts and sat back down. He had the letter. Opened it. His hands began to tremble again. He pulled out from the envelope a sheet of blue paper and recognized Olia's script from the notes he had seen on the back of her photos. It was too dark to read. He moved over to the nearest street lamp in front of the park fence. The light shone down on the paper and Olia's words.

44

THE STREET LAMP illuminated the paper and the black jackets. Their steel rods gleamed as they advanced towards Askia. They walked swiftly, and Askia's eyes were on the letter. From the shadow of a lone tree deep in the park came a melancholy birdsong. The first skinhead quickened his pace, and Askia knew he would not have time to finish the letter and at the same time that he could not accept what was happening without having read the letter.

The first skinhead was moving fast and Askia started to run. He clasped Olia's message against his chest.

Askia,

This is not a letter but an admission of failure. I
thought I would be able to stay, but it has taken
hold of me again. Already in Sofia we were the
Gypsies, the black-haired, dirty outsiders, with our
scattered world and our destiny bartered to the gods
of the caravan.

The skinheads were moving fast. Ahead, the
street was long and straight. The three men laughed
and blustered:

"Hey, boys, should we let him run for a bit?"

"The cops have been through this area. They
won't be back here for a while!"

"Keep running, nigger — that's something you
know how to do! Racing, like an Ethiopian marathon
runner!"

"Go on, run! Hey, what does your letter say?"

When I grew up, I didn't want to be the stranger
with the dirty hair. I ran away. And I started taking
photographs, putting together albums as a way to
tie together my pictures, my dispersed lives, all those
gobbled up by my Leica, as evidence of a failure.
Apparently the striving endures, the desire endures
— to create the connection, the bridge between the
different shores of our lives, our wandering lives.

There were no bends in the street, no cross streets or alleys where Askia might hide long enough to finish reading the letter. Just this street that would not end, and if there were side streets, he was running too hard to notice. If he turned his head right or left, the leather jackets would catch up with him. They seemed to have decided not to let him keep running, and a thought occurred to him — *Stop and negotiate*: "Guys, I just need a little time to read the letter. Then you can go ahead . . ."

Not to check out without having seen what Olia had written.

The forms of my prints, my life, my mornings, my nights are breaking apart. They're liquefying because they carry within them lines of conflict. My conflicts, my memory, shattered, lying in pieces along the roads of my escape.

And this endless asphalt that would not run out, this street that would not run its course but which began to narrow, to gradually turn into a corridor, and he told himself that if it became a bottleneck it would pressure them and they would put an end to the whole thing. His knees were about to give out. He felt it. It looked as if the black jackets were also beginning to tire. The front-runner complained,

"Hey! Marathon man! We didn't learn to run in the Kenyan mountains! We don't have specially baked feet! Stop so we can finish the job!"

The skinhead stopped running. Askia sensed this because no more footsteps echoed on the asphalt. The others must have followed his lead, and Askia thought he could finish reading the letter.

> *Askia, there is no constant in all of this. What our lives consist of is nothing but the gallery walls, the book pages where we sometimes happen to place a few pictures, an absurd story, while we wait for the echo, the response, while we hope to finally draw the line that threads us, others, the world together. Yet you see that the thread that could lead you back to the country you believe was your starting point and might hold out a more accurate image of who you are — that thread, you realize, has snapped. Your father's face, which I fixed on my rolls of film, has ultimately become dislocated, has broken up. There may be nothing left of him to salvage, so I think the time, the nighttime, has come to put an end to the flight.*

45

AT THE END of the night was Petite-Guinée's bistro. The long street had exhausted the black jackets. Behind the counter the barman was cleaning glasses.

"Whisky, Askia? Sorry, but I've already put away the Miles discs. You'll have to drink your whisky solo and neat. Without Miles."

" . . ."

He asked after Petite-Guinée. The barman said he had not seen the old man very much in the past few days. He stole in like a burglar, served himself a drink at the bar, and then disappeared into the belly of the cellar. He didn't feel like surfacing anymore. He didn't bother with the bistro anymore, and the barman had taken on duties that weren't usually his:

put in the orders, pay the bills, take reservations. He said he was worried about the boss, who had become a ghost.

Askia went behind the bar and took the stairs leading down to his friend's studio. The damp walls made him shiver. He stood in front of the cellar. Pushed at the door without knocking. He had never knocked on Petite-Guinée's door. He had always entered into the ex-mercenary's world as if it were his own house.

The door stayed shut. Locked. Petite-Guinée did not want to be disturbed. Askia remained on the steps. There were noises coming from the bar. Voices, a tone, the laugh of the skinhead who had followed him longer than the others. More voices . . . He did not go back up to the bar. He went down, and found himself in front of that other door, the one that opened into the cubbyhole that Petite-Guinée called his land of the depths. Walls, a universe, the large table on which he had spread out his souvenirs of Biafra, the photos, faces, smiles of the kids that he had latched on to as a final homeland.

Askia pushed the door. It swung open. The luminous strip of the fluorescent fixture hung from the ceiling. On the big dining table was Petite-Guinée, curled up, with a bottle in the hollow between his bent abdomen and folded knees, barefoot, one arm hidden under his side, the other rigid against the exposed side of his trunk. His frozen fingers had dropped a photograph next to his thigh. Askia stepped closer, picked up the photo: two children, a girl and a boy, laughing in a countryside. The note on the back read: *Biafra 1969*. Petite-Guinée had lain down on top of the other portraits, on the little snapshots that reminded him of Africa. Dead. Buried in a landscape, a distant land.

There was mayhem going on upstairs. The black jackets were drinking and smashing up Petite-Guinée's bar.

46

"WILL YOU FINALLY tell me who Askia is?" Olia had
pleaded with her eyes.

And he remembered his parents sighing. "At last!"
At last, after the roads and humiliations they had left
behind, they had made a little place for themselves in
Chief Gokoli's village during the winter of 1967. His
mother, Kadia Saran, sold kola nuts on the steps of
the German pastors' century-old school — the only
school there. His father, Sidi Ben Sylla Mohammed,
cultivated a plot of land in the hills to the east overlooking the village. In the evening he would come
home from the fields carrying the machete in his left
hand and the hoe on his right shoulder. The blade
of the hoe rubbed against the edges of his turban,

perpetually white, impervious to dirt. It was a mystery how he managed to keep it so immaculate. The fact that he wore it on his head could not explain why it stayed absolutely spotless. In the fields he walked under trees and bird nests laden with excrement. Besides, he was tall, and his head would unavoidably brush against the wet leaves and low branches. In the absence of an explanation, the rumour eventually spread that it was not the turban. It was his heart. His heart remained unsullied.

They spent three peaceful years in the village, though they continued to be the Dirty Feet. Until that season when rain was scarce on the plateaus, where it was plentiful as a rule. And the seers and wise men who were consulted, and the villagers, and all the signs in the sky concurred that the paucity of rain was due, without a doubt, to the Dirty Feet. Who must have been afflicted by a curse. It had been right to welcome them for a few days, but letting them settle there had not been the best idea in the world. And the village notables went to see Chief Gokoli. To ask him to send the strangers away.

"Chief, should we let them stay in the village, when all the signs and sages say . . ."

". . . that it is because of them the soil is dry and ungenerous this year?"

"Should we allow them to stay and watch our fields burn, our rivers and wells dry up?"

"Allow them to leave in their wake a hundred years of epidemics, many seasons of torment and tears?"

"Dead cities, knives of hate, the incessant groans of a woman pregnant with a three-horned child who will not leave her belly, a downpour of scorpions."

"Is it possible for our hospitality to be boundless and hence for us to let all these things take place?"

"Should we go on offering shelter to these charlatans, who will continue to destroy all our lands to the point of exhausting them and murdering the world?"

Thus they were forced to leave the village of Chief Gokoli. And ended up on the coast. His mother told him that his father, Sidi, had gone still farther, for reasons even more obscure. And she spoke of the letters from Paris. Askia never saw those letters. But why Paris? Was it because, as his mother had apparently learned one day — he did not know how — Paris was a Mecca where thousands of Dirty Feet arrived after exodus, roads, hunger? And the letters, did they exist only in his mother's fantasies, she who was at times more clear-sighted as to what had happened to Sidi? One day, Kadia Saran, her eyes fixed on the ocean shore, spoke these words: "Askia, he has abandoned us. To escape beyond the bounds of the Gulf of Guinea. I've been told that he embarked on an old tub called *Bonne Espérance* and that, at this very moment, he is in a South African diamond mine near Kimberley, where they say the precious stones engender fortunes, happiness, and wretchedness. I picture him, his dry body stooped over, digging in the dirt with a pickaxe. He wears a safety helmet and an orange suit because down there they have serious companies that know how to do things according to the rules. He is digging and hopes to find the biggest, most beautiful stone, which will earn him a reward from the mine owners. I imagine it happening this way, my son, because for thousands of seasons I have had no news from Sidi."

47

ASKIA REMAINED SEATED on the cellar floor. He wanted to keep vigil by his friend. The serenity and peacefulness of his face were striking. Petite-Guinée was happy. Now. Askia was sad that he was gone, but he had no right to be selfish. He rejoiced at this ultimate happiness that had come to Petite-Guinée. He wanted to hold this wake with joy in his heart, as was done for the righteous in his father's land. They say there that the wicked die forgotten and alone. That was not the case for Petite-Guinée. He died surrounded by the images and laughter of children. Askia guessed that his friend had begun by sitting on the table, chatting with the children in the photographs. He confessed to them that he had not realized he loved them but now he knew. He loved them. Then he had thanked them for populating the land of his cellar. And he had believed that in the eyes of the kids in the photos he could see their response. The kids had told him that the land of his cellar was the most beautiful they had ever inhabited. And Petite-Guinée, still sitting at one end of the big table, had been moved to tears.

He had spoken for a long time, and when he began to grow tired, Petite-Guinée lay down on his side. He had kept on conversing with the children. They told each other jokes. The children in the photos laughed at the jokes, and so did Petite-Guinée. They giggled happily. Had more fun than they had ever had. They felt good. Until his heart stopped beating.

Above Askia's head the mayhem continued. The black jackets were demolishing the bistro that Petite-Guinée had bought with his mercenary earnings. They tittered . . . The Wedding . . .

Askia watched over his friend and laughed out loud. The expression on the dead man's face had changed. He was radiant, and Askia envied his good fortune. He lay down on his side like the dead man and continued to laugh, hard, hoping that his heart would stop beating, that death would take him like a righteous man, bedded down on this cold floor. He chuckled for a good half-hour, but his heart would not give out. Above the cellar, the uproar diminished. The skinheads were taking a break and the barman was drowning in his own blood. The street was deserted.

48

OVERHEAD, THE BLACK jackets got back to work. The steel bars pulverized the counter. Askia was in the basement, but at the same time he had his hands on the steering wheel of his cab. He was not going to wait for the black jackets. He would turn the ignition key and press down on the accelerator. One last run. He was both the driver and the fare. He was ready, and so was the passenger. The passenger did not need to specify the address of his destination. He knew it. The destination and the street number were infinity. The night was sad.

To depart in his taxi, the site of his quest. Open the glove compartment and take out the cloth that served to clean the dashboard. Unlock the door, get out, and go to the back of the vehicle. Insert the cloth into the exhaust pipe. Remove his shoes, take off his socks, and stuff them into the exhaust as well. Go back to his seat, lock the door again, roll up the windows. His hands on the steering wheel.

The noise from the bar came down into the cellar. The black jackets were walking down the cold steps. Askia imagined his windshield, stared at the heavy door that stood between him and the stairway. He saw a screen, the one from his childhood, a picture at the foot of his bed, the same one where his father's silhouette would appear. There it was, the shadow of his father, Sidi Ben Sylla Mohammed, faithful, impressive in the night, through the windshield. The shadow was not threatening. It faced him and played with a clown, who had large wings on his back.

Sidi was looking at him. Askia knew what he must do. Tilt the seat back, close his eyes, turn on the ignition.

The black jackets swung their steel bars against the door of the land of the cellar, Petite-Guinée's tomb — what is referred to as a profanation. An event like the most mundane sort of news item: the steel bars and the boots smashing the tombstone. On their lips, a battle song. The three men unzipped their pants and pissed on what was left of the stone. After which they lowered their pants and emptied their bowels on the broken sepulchre and on the remains of a body that had no right to be there. The leader of the group pulled out a spray can and drew a cross on the stone. A cross in the shape of a swastika. Once the cross was done, a salute: right arm extended and raised to a god far away. Or close by.

Askia wished that Olia would thump on the back door and ask if she could come along for the ride. The engine thrummed; he sensed the girl sitting in the back. She was there. She stuck her head out the open window and photographed the passersby: men, women, children pursued by evil people. People who caught them, raped them, cut their throats, dismembered them, and then displayed their pariah heads like trophies.

The engine coughed. In front of Askia, a brutal shaft of light pierced the windshield, the cellar door. The shaft of light burned the door, blowing it to pieces. The black jackets and steel bars started once again to strike. And the little scamps from the garbage dump in Trois-Collines finally killed Pontos, Father Lem's dog, which was not entitled to join in their games.

Acknowledgements

The translator is grateful to the Centre national du livre (France) and to the Canada Council for the Arts for their financial assistance.

About the Author

EDEM AWUMEY was born in Togo in 1975. His first novel, *Port-Mélo*, won the Grand prix littéraire d'Afrique noire, one of the most distinguished literary prizes in Africa, and his second novel, the French edition of *Dirty Feet* (*Les pieds sales*), was a finalist for one of France's most prestigious literary prizes, the Prix Goncourt. Awumey now lives in Canada, where he is a teacher.

About the Translator

LAZER LEDERHENDLER's translations of contemporary Québécois fiction have garnered distinctions and nominations for literary prizes in Canada and the UK. His translation of Nicolas Dickner's *Nikolski* won the Governor General's Literary Award as well as the Quebec Writers' Federation Award, and his translation of Gaétan Soucy's *The Immaculate Conception* was a finalist for the Scotiabank Giller Prize and won the Quebec Writers' Federation Award. He lives in Montreal.